Grover Shipton
1928

Grover
Shipton

" THE EGG IS HATCHING—I HEARD IT—SO DID THE CAP'N ! "

Jerry Todd and the Purring Egg. *Frontispiece—(Page 88)*

JERRY TODD AND THE PURRING EGG

BY

LEO EDWARDS

AUTHOR OF
THE JERRY TODD BOOKS, ETC.

ILLUSTRATED BY
BERT SALG

GROSSET & DUNLAP
PUBLISHERS : : NEW YORK

Made in the United States of America

To

HERB AND EUGENE

JERRY TODD SAYS:

JUST think how excited you'd be to start out in the morning a poor kid with patches on the seat of your pants and come home at night a young millionaire. Sounds like a fairy story, hey? Well, that is what happens to me in this story of mystery and hilarious adventure. Boy, the fun I was going to have with my fortune, I said.

But I wasn't stingy with my new wealth. I remembered my chums. Scoop, Red and Peg each got fifty thousand dollars. Also I gave old Cap'n Tinkertop ten thousand dollars. In one day I spent one hundred and sixty thousand dollars out of my million dollars.

What was the humpback's secret? Why was he hiding nights in the Cap'n's barn? Why did he set fire to the barn? And, as amazing as anything else, though a small thing in itself, why did he come back to the barn after the fire, while we were in the haymow where the pool of blood was, to steal a common china nest egg?

There *is* mystery and shivers in this story.

Br-r-r-r-r! Caught alone once, I thought I was done for. Yet we had crazy fun in the adventure too, like the night we abducted Humpty-Dumpty, the rejuvenated dodo egg taken from King Tut's tomb. That was the *craziest* scheme ever—abducting an egg! And while hidden in the spooky cellar we heard those same queer padded footsteps over our heads. *Pat! . . . Pat! . . .Pat!* . . . Creepy, I'll tell the world. For it was in the dead of night.

Then came a gurgling scream. Old Cap'n Tinkertop! A "hairy" catchup bottle had jumped at him, he told us, dizzy after his mysterious attack. A "hairy" catchup bottle; a hair-lined cave nest! What was the hidden connection? Was it a dodo hen's nest? Were the eggs we found real dodo eggs? The story tells in rollicking style. You'll laugh your head off one minute and shiver the next.

This is my sixth JERRY TODD book. The titles of my other books in their order are:

JERRY TODD AND THE WHISPERING MUMMY

JERRY TODD AND THE ROSE-COLORED CAT

JERRY TODD AND THE OAK ISLAND TREASURE

JERRY TODD AND THE WALTZING HEN

JERRY TODD AND THE TALKING FROG

My seventh book will be about a mysterious man with a strange "sleeping toe." Remember our show boat, *The Sally Ann,* in my third book, JERRY TODD AND THE OAK ISLAND TREASURE? Well, we went back to the island in our clever little ark to empty a bee tree. There we found the Rev. Joshua Jonathan Jacobs living in a hidden cave.

What was the secret of the cave's sighing, whispering voice? Was the black toe on the white man's foot a cannibal's toe, as he said? Was the toe actually hypnotized? We thought the man's story was bunk. He was trying to string us, we said. But an amazing thing happened when the toe "woke up." Boy, it was a narrow escape for me!

A real shipwreck, just like in a sea story, a tub raft patterned after the one in the *Swiss Family Robinson* book, cannibals, wild battles on an isolated island, hidden treasure, a smart rich kid who thought he owned the earth—plenty of material here for a corking good fun-mystery-adventure story. So watch for my seventh book, JERRY TODD IN THE WHISPERING CAVE.

Your friend,

JERRY TODD.

CONTENTS

JERRY TODD AND THE PURRING EGG

CHAPTER I

THE EGG IN THE CAVE

THIS story starts in a cave in Higbee's ravine. I was in the cave hunting for crystals. I guess you know what a crystal is. It's like a hunk of glass only it isn't glass. As much as I've hunted for crystals in the caves near Tutter, where I live, I've never found one. I guess I never will find one. But crystal hunting is fun, anyway.

I had a candle. For it was dark in the cave where I was. And all of a sudden I saw something at my feet that made my eyes pop. It was a great big egg. Say, it was a whopper. There it lay in a sort of hollowed-out sand nest. I was excited, I want to tell you. A hundred crystals wouldn't have excited me half as much as this big egg. I knew I had made a big find.

A dinosaur egg—that's what it was. I could think of nothing else.

I ran back to the mouth of the cave.

"Hey!" I yipped to my three chums, who were playing leapfrog in the bed of the ravine. "Come quick! I've found something."

"It must be a gold mine," said Peg Shaw, coming on the run with the other two leapfroggers.

"Or a hunk of licorice," panted Red Meyers.

Peg Shaw is the biggest one in our four-cornered gang. Red is the smallest. We call him Red because he has red hair and freckles. I've got freckles, too. But I haven't got red hair. I'm glad of that.

"Say," I cried, "did you fellows see in the newspaper the other day about Roy Chapman Andrews' dinosaur eggs?"

"No," said Peg. "What about it?"

"Well, I've found one, too."

"Found one what?"

"A dinosaur egg."

Scoop Ellery laughed in ridicule.

"Aw, Jerry. Tell that to the marines. There never was any dinosaurs around here. I read that newspaper article about Mr. Andrews. He found his petrified dinosaur eggs over in China. And *this* isn't China. It's Illinois."

"There's one here in the cave," I declared.

"In *that* cave?" Scoop pointed, and then he laughed some more. "You poor fish! Don't you know that a dinosaur is as big as a house? Why, sure thing it is. A dinosaur, let me tell you, is as big as the Methodist Church. So how could it have gotten into a little cave like that?"

"I don't know how it did it," I cried, "but the egg is there. That's enough for me. And it's worth five thousand dollars, too. For that's what Mr. Andrews got for his dinosaur eggs."

Peg put his head in the cave and let out four or five inches of neck.

"Come on with your candle," said he. "I want to see this wonderful egg."

Pretty soon we came to the sand nest.

"There," I pointed in triumph. "I guess you fellows won't laugh at me now."

Peg gave the big egg a kick.

"Nothing but a stone," he grunted.

"It's petrified," I told him, remembering what the newspaper had said about the eggs that Mr. Andrews had found.

"So is your head," he laughed.

"But look at the shape," I hung on. "It's a perfect egg. You can see that, can't you?"

"It looks like an egg," said Scoop, after he

had examined it. "But it isn't—not even a petrified egg. As Peg says, it's nothing but a queer-shaped stone."

"But how did it get here?" I cried, disappointed. "And how about the nest?"

"Search me how it got here," said Scoop, shrugging. "But it isn't an egg—that's one sure thing."

I groaned.

"It's awful," I said, "to have five thousand dollars and lose it that easy. I thought I was going to be rich."

"Now that we've got it," laughed Peg, giving the big egg another kick, "what are we going to do with it?"

"I found it," I said. "It ought to be mine by rights. But if you fellows want it you can have it. I don't want to be piggy."

"Help yourself," said Red Meyers. "I wouldn't lug it home for fifty cents."

"Yah," put in Scoop, with a liberal gesture. "It's yours, Jerry. Take it home and hatch it if you can."

"It's a curiosity," I told the others, "and I'm going to keep it."

The leader thought he could have some fun with me.

"Who knows," he laughed, "but what it will turn out to be a real dinosaur egg after all."

"It might at that," said Peg.

"And if Jerry hatches it," added the leader, "he'll be the father of the only dinosaur in captivity."

"We'll help you bring up your baby, Jerry," offered Red.

"Sure thing," laughed Scoop. "I'll be its godfather if you'll let me. And when it has the tummy ache I'll help you dose it with castor oil."

"Jerry's going to be famous," said Peg.

"And rich," said Scoop.

Red jiggled my arm, trying to make me drop the big egg. "Watch out there, old kid. Don't drop your fortune and crack it."

"If you fellows don't dry up," I threatened, "one of you will get this egg on his bean."

Scoop drew his face down.

"No kidding, Jerry," said he, "but are you going to tell Mr. Stair about your dinosaur egg?"

"Mr. Stair?" I repeated.

"The editor of the Tutter newspaper. He'll think this egg is a big piece of news. See? And I bet you he'll have your name spread all over the front page of his newspaper. You'll be as famous as Mr. Andrews."

Peg laughed.

"Let's not tell the newspaper man about our egg. Let's keep it a secret. Maybe we can have some fun with it."

"What kind of fun?" inquired Scoop.

"The egg fooled Jerry. So why can't we fool other people?"

"I'd like to fool Bid Stricker," said Red, speaking the name of the leader of the Zulutown gang. "For he's always butting in on us. And it would be fun to make a monkey of him."

We haven't any use for the Zulutown gang, especially Bid, the leader. He's a roughneck and his whole gang are roughnecks.

"I know how we can fool Bid," said Peg. "We'll bury the egg in some gravel pit, along with a lot of old horse-bones. Then we'll make up a story that will start Bid and his gang to digging in the gravel with picks and shovels. When they uncover the bones and the egg they'll think it's a real dinosaur egg. See?"

"If you want to fool somebody," I spoke up, "why don't you go after old Cap'n Tinkertop? We owe him something, anyway, for the trick he played on me the day he had me chasing all over town after a kitchen wrench."

"Hot dog!" cried Peg, his eyes dancing. "I never thought of the Cap'n."

"He's interested in eggs," I added.

"Hen eggs," said Red.

"We'll tell him this is a goofle egg," I laughed.

Scoop chuckled.

"Did I tell you the joke I played on the old man to-day?"

"No. What was it?"

"I figured he had something coming to him for the kitchen-wrench trick. So this morning when he came in the store to buy a dozen fresh eggs I sold him six hen eggs and six china eggs."

"Nest eggs?" laughed Peg.

"Sure thing."

"He'll come back to the store and bounce the china eggs on your bean," I told the leader. "For you know his temper. He hasn't any sense when he gets mad."

"I should worry," shrugged Scoop. "If I see him coming I'll duck. He won't get *me*. Not to-day, kid, nor to-morrow, either."

Starting for home, we took turns carrying the big egg. It was pretty heavy. I guess it weighed eight or ten pounds. I sort of measured it in carrying it and found that it was bigger around than I could span and touch with my fingers and thumbs. And from one end to the other it was fully eight inches. In shape, as I have said, it was a perfect egg. Nature certainly had done a good job on it. I couldn't help wondering if it wasn't a petrified egg, after all.

Coming into town, we hurried through Zulutown, which is the name that the Tutter people have for the tough section of town beyond Dad's brickyard. Bid Stricker lives in Zulutown. The Cap'n, too. So in the interests of our coming trick we kept our big egg out of sight. For we didn't want either the Cap'n or Bid to see it. That would spoil our fun—though just what our trick was going to be we hadn't determined.

Pretty soon I turned into our yard. Mother was in the kitchen getting supper. Her warm smile turned into a stare when she saw what I was carrying.

"Goodness gracious!" she cried. "Is it an egg?"

"A goofle egg," I joked.

"Well, you can 'goofle' it outside," said she, sort of shooing me toward the door. "For there's enough of your truck scattered throughout the house as it is."

I saw a chance to have some fun with her.

"Why can't we keep it in the parlor?" I said.

"*That* thing?"

"I can paint it pink with green spots," I said, earnest-like. "It'll look awful pretty."

"Jerry! It's a wonder to me that you don't want to lug in an armful of your father's paving bricks and paint them red, white and blue."

"It's a curiosity," I defended, continuing my joke.

"Of course it is. But this is no museum."

While I was washing my face and hands in the kitchen sink Dad came into the room, whistling and jiggling his feet in time to the music. In hugging Mother he reached behind and untied her apron strings. Then he gave me a swat on the head with the evening newspaper. When it comes to being lively and full of fun I'll put my dad up against any other man in La Salle County. He's great!

"Well, well," said he, getting his eyes on my big stone egg. "Who says the hens aren't laying this summer?"

"It isn't a hen egg," I grinned. "It's a goofle egg."

"How do we eat it?"

"We don't eat it," I said.

"No?"

"It's just a stone," I explained.

"And can you imagine," Mother sputtered, when Dad got in her way, "Jerry actually wants to paint it pink with green spots and put it in the parlor!"

"Fine!" laughed Dad, giving me the wink. "I always said that home wasn't complete without a pink and green goofle egg. I think we're pretty lucky to have one. Yes, sir-ee! Think of all the poor families who can't afford to own a goofle egg."

"It'll look swell on the piano beside Aunt Hattie's wedding picture," I said.

"Let me catch you putting it on the piano," sputtered Mother, "and something will happen to you, young man."

Here Dad thought of something.

"Speaking of goofle eggs," said he, "reminds me that I have a message for you, Jerry."

"Yes?" I said.

"It's from Cap'n Tinkertop."

"That silly old bachelor!" sputtered Mother, fussing with her apron strings. "I can't understand what the boys see in him. I sometimes wish Jerry didn't go there so much."

"The Cap'n's all right," I defended.

Dad looked at me and laughed.

"You didn't think so the day he had you chasing all over town after a kitchen wrench. Hey?"

I grinned, sheepish-like.

"Who told you about the kitchen wrench?" I inquired.

"Oh, I found out about it," he laughed. "I didn't think you were so dumb, Jerry."

"Just the same," I waggled, "the Cap'n's all right, even if he does play tricks on us. For when we're at his house he lets us do anything we want to do."

"Yes," said Mother, "Mrs. Meyers told me how you and Donald baked biscuits the day you had dinner in Zulutown. . . . Did you actually *eat* them?"

I stared at her. That was a queer thing for her to ask. What would we do with them if we didn't eat them? It was like asking what good is a clock, or why does a cow breathe.

"The Cap'n," followed up Dad, "was peg-legging for the depot when I saw him. He was on his way to Ashton, he said, to get a new thing-um-bob for his incubator. He may be away all night. So he wants you to take care of his incubator until he gets back."

"Has he got eggs in it?"

"Sure thing."

"I don't know anything about incubators," I said.

"Oh," laughed Dad, "I've got the whole dope for you. All you've got to do is to listen to me and do as I tell you. You're to go over to his barn after supper and see that the incubator is kept at a hundred and three. There's a thermometer to go by. And you regulate the temperature by raising or lowering the wick of the incubator lamp. See? If the Cap'n doesn't come home on number seven you're to take the eggs out of the incubator at ten-thirty and give them a bath in lukewarm water."

"I'll get Scoop to help me," I said.

Dad nodded.

"Yes," said he, "the Cap'n mentioned Scoop."

CHAPTER II

TOMATO "SOUP"

WHEN supper was over I hunted up Scoop, telling him about my job, and the two of us headed for Zulutown. As we turned into the Cap'n's yard Bid Stricker, who lives close by, came into sight. I don't remember what he said to us, but it was something smart. That's the kind of a kid *he* is. It's no wonder we have it in for him.

"He's still out there in the Cap'n's yard," said Scoop, when we had gone into the barn where the incubator was.

I got my nose to a crack in the barn's wooden wall.

"There comes Jimmy Stricker," I pointed, naming Bid's smaller cousin.

"I can see Hib Milden, too," said Scoop.

"One, two, three, four, five," I counted. "Look! Bid's telling the gang something about us—he's pointing this way."

"Maybe they're going to attack us," said

Scoop. "Let's get the door closed and lock ourselves in."

Pretty soon there was a bang! bang! of rocks on the side of the barn. But that didn't worry us. We were safe. And we had a lot of fun yelling stuff at the rock throwers.

"I wish, though," said Scoop, during the bombardment, "that *we* had some rocks, too. Then we'd show them that this is a game that two sides can play at."

"I'd rather have a stack of rotten eggs," I laughed. "Oh, boy! Wouldn't it be fun to paste Bid with a nice ripe egg! One that had been laying around in the sun for a month or two."

Five or ten minutes passed. It was quiet outside the barn now. The yard was deserted. Having failed in their attack on us, the enemy had vanished.

"But let's not be fooled," said Scoop, using his head. "They may be up to some kind of a trick. You know Bid. Before we open the door we'll make sure that they've gone."

As I say, the Cap'n's incubator was in the barn. And now, in the quiet following the enemy's attack, we gave the home-made egg hatcher some attention. Dad had said that we were to keep the thermometer at a hundred and three. We found that the thermometer was all right. So there was nothing for us to do except to wait around until the old man came home on the ten-thirty train.

Now, ten-thirty isn't late. Lots of nights I've been up until eleven or twelve o'clock. I can remember a few nights when I stayed up even later than that. But watching an incubator isn't very exciting sport. And as it got close to ten o'clock we had a fight on our hands to keep the sleep out of our eyes.

"Ho-hum!" yawned Scoop, stretching. "I'm pretty near asleep, Jerry."

"Me, too," I yawned.

"It looks foolish to me staying here. The incubator's all right."

"The Cap'n wouldn't have asked us to stay," I said, "if it wasn't important."

"Do you suppose he's testing the incubator?"

"Probably. He's been working on it for weeks. You know that."

"Huh!" grunted Scoop, turning up his nose at the home-made egg hatcher. "It doesn't look like much of an invention to me. All it is is a box with a lamp in it."

"The Cap'n thinks it's a very wonderful invention," I said.

"Yah, he told me how he was going to get it patented and make a fortune."

"I hope he does," I waggled.

I was thinking at the moment how very poor the Cap'n was. And I was thinking, too, how bully it would be if he *did* get a fortune out of his invention.

It was years and years ago that the old man first came to Tutter. He was a canal-boat captain then. That was before I was born. We don't have canal boats in and through Tutter now. They sort of went out of business. I guess they were too slow. Anyway, the Cap'n found himself out of a job. And because he had lost a leg at the knee he was given a small monthly pension. He lives in one of Dad's houses in Zulutown.

Scoop and I kept on yawning and stretching. Then the leader went to the door and squinted outside into the moonlit yard.

"I wonder if the Strickers are still laying for us."

"You don't see them?"

"No."

"Anyway," I said, "they'd be hid."

"Sure thing. . . . Say, Jerry, I've got a notion to do some scouting."

"If they catch you," I said, "they'll paste you good and proper."

"Oh, I won't let them catch me. They aren't smart enough for that. Lock the door when I go out. When I want to come in I'll whisper 'eggs.' See?"

Left alone in the silent, shadowy barn I suddenly got the queer, shaky feeling that I was being watched. I don't know what gave me that feeling—certainly I hadn't heard anything or seen anything to alarm me. But, as I say, the feeling came to me suddenly.

I had a lantern. And turning up the wick as high as it would stand without smoking, I took a look around the barn. There was nobody in the lower part of the building. I was sure of that.

The haymow! I looked up quickly, expecting to see a face in the opening at the head of the ladder. But there was no face there. And still the barn, both above and below, was as silent as a tomb. I was shivering now.

I ran to the door when I heard Scoop. But I forgot my scare when I saw what he was carrying.

"Hot dog!" he laughed. "I fooled Bid Stricker that time. Say, I pulled a clever one on him. Brag on me, kid. I deserve it."

"Is Bid out there?" I whispered.

"Sure thing. The whole gang is parked in the weeds. They're waiting for us to start for home. Ripe tomatoes! That's what they had for us. But they haven't got the tomatoes now. For I crawled up on them and swiped their juicy ammunition. Lookit! Here's a whole bagful."

I got a big juicy tomato out of the bag.

"Oh, mamma!" I cried, winding up my throwing arm. "I'd like to squash this in Bid's face."

The leader was as eager for a battle as I was.

"That's the stuff, Jerry," he laughed. "Get your arm limbered up. Are you ready? Here we go."

Gee! I like to think of the fun we had that night. We loaded up with tomatoes. I had ten or twelve, I guess. Nice big juicy fellows. I could imagine how they would squash and splatter when they struck. Scoop had a supply, too. And thus armed we let ourselves out of the barn and crawled toward the enemy.

We could hear low voices now.

"I wonder if they're going to stay in the barn all night," Bid grumbled to his gang.

Hib Milden snickered.

"They'll wish they'd stayed in the barn forever when they get our tomatoes. Sweet doctor!

I've been waiting for this chance to soak Jerry Todd. That kid thinks he's smart."

"Huh!" grunted Bid. "How about Scoop Ellery?"

"They both need some tomato soup," laughed Jimmy Stricker.

"Yah," said Hib, "and they're both going to get it, bu-lieve me."

Scoop nudged me in the ribs.

"Tomato soup, Jerry!"

"They'll think it's tomato soup," I giggled, "when we land on them."

"You tell 'em, kid."

"Shall we soak 'em now?" I breathed in his ear.

"No need to hurry," he whispered back. "Let's lay and listen to their gab for a few minutes. This 'tomato soup' talk of theirs is funny."

Hib was the next one to speak up.

"What's their idea in staying in the barn?" he grunted.

"They're taking care of the Cap'n's incubator," Bid explained.

"Why doesn't he take care of it himself?"

"He isn't here. He went over to Ashton this afternoon."

"Huh!" grunted Hib. "They're his pets."

"I heard him talking with Jerry's pa," said Bid. "That's how I came to know that Jerry was going to be here to-night."

There was a moment's silence. And creeping closer, I got a glimpse of the enemy in the weeds. The moon showed them up. But we were careful that the same moon didn't show *us* up.

"How many tomatoes have you got?" inquired Hib.

"A whole bagful," said Bid. "I swiped all Mrs. Maloney had in her garden."

Hib got on his knees and moved around.

"I can't find the bag."

"It's there where you are."

"Like so much mud."

"It was there a moment ago."

"Well, it isn't here now."

Scoop snickered.

"We know where the bag is. Eh, Jerry?"

"Tomato soup," I whispered back.

Bid and his gang were stirring around now.

"What do you know about that!" said the leader, excited-like. "The bag's gone."

Scoop pinched my arm.

"Get ready, Jerry. I'll take the Stricker cousins and Hib. You take the other two. Soak 'em good. Then skin back to the barn."

I took aim. Bing! My man got it square on the back of the head. Boy, did that old tomato ever squash and splatter! In the same moment Bid got one on the neck.

"How do you like that?" yipped Scoop, slamming away with his ammunition. "You will lay for us, hey? Pretty good tomatoes, hey? You took all Mrs. Maloney had, hey? They sure make swell tomato soup."

"Yah," I yipped, "how do you like *our* kind of tomato soup? Pretty good stuff, hey?"

"Sock 'em, Jerry!"

"Bu-lieve me I am soaking 'em," I cried, pumping away.

There was an awful howl from the splattered enemy.

"We'll get you for this!" yelled Bid, coughing up a pack of tomato seeds.

"Oh! . . ." gurgled Hib. "I got one in the mouth."

"Your mouth's so big we couldn't miss it," I yelled.

"Swallow this one," cried Scoop, letting fly.

"Oh! . . ." howled Hib, clawing at the gob on his face.

Well, we ran the smart Alecks out of the yard. That wasn't hard to do. For they haven't much grit. Besides, we had the upper hand of them now. They managed to find a few rocks. But we had ten times as much ammunition as they had.

Coming out victorious in the fight, and proud of it, we scooted back to the barn.

"Lookit!" cried Scoop, in sudden amazement. "The barn's on fire!"

We dashed inside, finding that the incubator had been tipped over in our absence. It was the escaping kerosene, used in the lamp, that had set fire to the barn floor.

Well, we stamped on the fire and put it out. Then we got the incubator up. Its legs were all right. Nothing was broken or disconnected. So we knew that the incubator hadn't tumbled over of its own accord. Some one had tipped it over.

I told Scoop then about my scare.

"There was some one in the haymow," I declared.

The leader grabbed the lantern.

"Come on," he gritted, starting for the ladder.

I don't mind telling you that I had a wabble in my legs as I followed the leader up the ladder into the haymow. I had the feeling that we were doing something risky. For if there was a man up there of an evil turn of mind he would have us at a disadvantage. And certainly he must be of an evil turn of mind, I concluded, to set fire to the barn.

But the haymow was empty.

"It must have been some tramp," Scoop concluded. "While we were out fighting the Strickers he beat it."

"But why did he tip the incubator over?" I puzzled.

"Search me," shrugged the leader.

I had the lantern now. And suddenly I made a discovery.

"Lookit!" I cried, pointing to the haymow floor.

What I had discovered was a pool of blood on the hay-covered floor. It wasn't dry blood—when I touched it I got red finger tips.

We had proof now that some one had been in the haymow—some one who was injured and bleeding. It could have been a tramp, as Scoop had said, for tramps had been known to sleep in the Cap'n's barn. But why, we asked ourselves, puzzled, had the injured tramp tried to burn the barn down?

It was a mystery, sort of.

CHAPTER III

THE VANISHED EGG

THE Strickers didn't come back that night. They didn't have the nerve. It was all right for them to sneak up on us when we weren't watching. They could do that easy enough. But now that we were wise to their tricks, and on our guard, they decided it was safest for them to keep out of our reach.

It was ten-thirty now. The Ashton accommodation had been in for twenty minutes or more. Yet the Cap'n hadn't showed up. So we were led to the conclusion that he intended to be away all night.

He had left word for us to take the eggs out of the incubator at ten-thirty and give them a bath in lukewarm water. And while we had the feeling, in what had happened to the incubator, that the eggs were now a broken mess, still we felt we had better carry out the old man's instructions as best we could. We would have to explain things to him later on; and it would help us considerably to be able to tell him that we had tried to carry out his instructions.

But the inside of the incubator wasn't a mess of broken eggs, as we had imagined it would be. In fact there were only six eggs in the tray. These eggs looked kind of queer to me—sort of shiny like a white doorknob. I held the lantern close to them. And when I got the truth of the situation I felt like two cents.

"We're a fine pair of wooden-headed boobs," I told the leader. "Lookit! Here's your six china eggs."

I wish you could have seen the expression on Scoop's face. He thinks he's pretty smart. And it galls him like sixty to be caught in a trick.

"Jerry," he swallowed, "the old man's sharper than I thought. He worked it pretty slick, didn't he? If he had asked *me* to come here I would have suspected a trick. So he got you."

I was angry.

"Yeh," I growled, "he used me to get even with you."

"What was it he told your pa?"

"He said I was to get you to come along and keep me company, as it would be kind of lonesome here by myself."

The other managed to laugh.

"Pretty slick."

I gritted my teeth at the incubator. For its glass panels reminded me of the Cap'n's crafty eyes.

"Let's get out of here," I growled, ready to quit.

Scoop jerked his head in his thoughts.

"Just the same," said he, "the old man might have lost his barn in this trick if we hadn't been here to put out the fire."

"We'll tell him about it."

"Maybe we ought to tell Bill Hadley, too."

I looked up.

"The town marshal?"

The leader nodded.

"Doesn't it strike you, Jerry, that there's something *wrong* about that pool of blood?"

"You think it's a mystery?"

"It's queer and out of the ordinary that an injured man should be hiding here in the hay-mow. Who was he? Why was he hiding here? Was he a law breaker? Was he shot by a police-man, or some one, in making an escape? That could be the case. He might even be a *mur-derer*."

I shivered.

"But what puzzles me more than anything else,"

the leader went on, "is why he tipped over the incubator."

"Maybe he wanted to burn up the barn so that no one would find out about the blood on the floor."

Scoop considered.

"Or it may have been the incubator that he wanted to destroy."

"But why should he want to burn up the incubator?"

"He may be an inventor. See? He may be working on an incubator like the Cap'n's. And wanting to get his own incubator patented first, he came here to burn up the other one."

"Aw, that's just a wild guess."

"It's a possibility. And when you're working on a mystery you've got to think of everything."

Well, we talked some more. To one point, we were sure that the Stricker gang was in no way responsible for the fire. For Bid and his gang had been outside in the weeds when the fire started. Besides we knew a kid wouldn't deliberately set fire to a building.

Before leaving for home we climbed the ladder into the haymow to take another look at the bloody floor. The blood was dry now. Hoping that we would find a clew of some sort, we made a thorough search of the haymow. But we found no clews. And giving up the search as useless we went below.

My eyes fell on the china eggs.

"If we could only think of some scheme to get back at the Cap'n," I gritted, my anger coming up again.

"Don't you worry, Jerry," the leader laughed. "He'll get his. I'll tell the world!"

"We ought to make it an egg trick."

"Leave it to me, kid. I'll think up something."

My eyes suddenly widened.

"Hey!" I cried. "Where's the other egg?"

"What other egg?"

"There was six china eggs. Now there's only five."

"*I* haven't got it."

"Nor me."

We searched the barn floor. But we couldn't find the missing egg. And in the end we were forced to the conclusion that the egg had been stolen while we were in the haymow the second time. As to the identity of the thief we could not doubt that it was the mysterious man who had been hiding in the haymow.

We were getting befuddled now.

"I could understand it," said Scoop, "if the man had stolen the incubator. That has some value. But what can be his idea in stealing a five-cent nest egg? Or, if he wanted one egg, why didn't he take all six of them?"

"Gosh!" I cried. "Don't ask *me*."

"Jerry, there's something queer about this."

"Let's beat it," I shivered.

"Maybe we ought to stand guard here to-night."

"Nothing doing," I shivered. "Me for home sweet home."

The other got his thoughts arranged.

"A mysterious hidden man," he murmured; "a pool of fresh blood; a fire; a vanished nest egg. . . . I wish I could put the puzzle together."

I yawned and shivered at the same time.

"It's going to eleven o'clock," I said. "So let's go home and get some sleep. If there's a mystery here we can tackle it to-morrow morning. Maybe, though, the Cap'n will be able to clear up everything when he gets home."

We left the barn then. It was still moonlight. That was a good thing and a bad thing. Danger couldn't creep up on us. But on the other hand the bright moonlight made us an easy target for hidden eyes.

Boy, was I ever glad to get into the street!

"Come on," I chattered, and down the sidewalk I went on the run.

CHAPTER IV

HUMPTY-DUMPTY

I'M like Dad. If I go to bed at night with a worry I sort of sleep it off. So I had no grouch in my mind the following morning when I uncovered my eyes to a recollection of the Cap'n's incubator trick. Instead, I got out of bed whistling and singing.

And what a wonderful morning it was! The lawn beneath my bedroom window was puddled with sunshine. I counted five robins and a crow. They sang very beautifully, only I don't know for sure whether the crow sang or not. Anyway, it was there.

As I dressed I went over in my mind our adventure in the Cap'n's barn. I had been scared in the dark. But I wasn't scared now. Not a particle. That is what the daylight does for a fellow. It takes away his shivers and makes him brave and daring. More than anything else I now wanted to get to work in that barn. I had the feeling, from what had happened, that there was a secret there. And I was crazy to find out what the secret was.

But maybe, I thought, I would find the barn in ruins. Maybe the mysterious man had returned in the dead of night to finish the job of burning the barn down. One thing sure, if the barn *had* been destroyed it would be my duty, and Scoop's, too, to go to Bill Hadley, the Tutter marshal, with an account of our adventure. If there was a fire-bug in town the law ought to know about it.

Having gotten into my clothes, I ran down the stairs to the dining-room where breakfast was ready for me.

"You can be 'pa' this morning," Mother smiled at me, motioning me to Dad's vacant chair at the sugar-bowl side of the table.

I remembered then that this was the week of the brickmakers' convention at Indianapolis. As a brickmaker Dad, of course, would attend the convention. When anything like that is going on he's always there. And that is what Mother meant by saying that I could be "pa." She meant that Dad was going to be away.

It is an honor to be "pa." Sometimes it means extra work, such as taking care of the furnace in the winter and shoveling snow. But I don't mind that. For the more work I do the more Dad appreciates me when he gets home. A fellow can work hard if he knows he's going to be handed a little praise.

Dad wasn't in the house, so I took it for granted that he had left for Indianapolis on the early-morning milk train. But Mother told me he was at the factory. Something had happened to the big brick-making machine, she said, and the night foreman had telephoned to the house for Dad to jump into his clothes and come quick.

"But he plans to leave on the eleven-thirty train," I was told in conclusion. "So you'd better be here, Jerry, as he'll want to say good-by to you."

Shortly after breakfast I was called to the telephone.

"Who is it?" I inquired.

"Six china eggs," came a deep mumbling voice.

"Huh!" I grunted, recognizing Scoop.

There was a giggle over the line.

"You don't like to hear about it, do you, Jerry?"

"I didn't lose any sleep over it," I grunted.

"Dog-gone him! He sure worked it slick.

But we'll fix him for his trick. I've got a hum-dinger of a scheme. Boy, it's a pippin."

"Tell me first," I said, "did the man come back and burn the barn down?"

"I didn't hear the fire truck out last night. So I guess the barn's safe."

"We were a couple of scaredy-calves," I said.

"We? Hey! How do you get that 'we' stuff?"

"Don't kid yourself," I laughed. "I didn't run home any faster than you did."

"I did that to keep you company."

"Oh, yes!"

"I saw you were scared. And I was afraid if I left you alone you'd get excited and turn into the wrong alley."

"I don't feel scared now," I told him. "And as soon as I get the chance I'm going to do some daylight investigating in that barn. For I've got a hunch there's a secret there.

"A bloody secret, hey?"

"You tell 'em."

"Say, Jerry."

"Yah?"

"Did I tell you I telephoned to Doc Leland?"

"What for?"

"Well, the man in the haymow was bleeding.

That was proof that he had some kind of an injury. And I figured that maybe he would go to Doc's office to have his injury dressed."

"Did you find out anything?"

"No. Doc said he hadn't had a stranger in his office in a week."

"Maybe the man is dead. Maybe he bled to death."

"Oh, I don't think so."

"He left a lot of blood in the haymow."

"I hope he left something else."

"What?"

"Footprints."

"In the blood?"

"Sure thing."

"We didn't see any footprints last night."

"Our light was poor. We ought to have better success in the daylight."

"How about the Cap'n?" I then inquired. "Are you going to tell him that a mysterious man was in his haymow last night?"

The other laughed.

"The less we tell the Cap'n just now the better."

"What do you mean?"

"Didn't I tell you a moment ago that I had a scheme in mind? Oh, boy! We're going to make the old man sorry for that china-egg trick. Say, Jerry."

"Yes?"

"Where's your big egg?"

"The one I found in the cave?"

"Sure thing."

"It's in the basement."

"Fine! Now, listen! Wrap it up so no one will see it and sneak it over to Red's house. I'll be along in a jiffy."

I let out a tickled yip. For I saw right off that it was the leader's scheme to fool the Cap'n with my goofle egg. I was glad now that I had brought the egg home. I had showed good sense in doing that. The other fellows had made fun of me when I kept the egg. But now they wanted to use it.

It is only a few doors from our house to Red's. And wrapping a newspaper around the big egg to hide it, I cut across the lawn. Peg was there when I got there. And he and Red pretty nearly giggled their heads off when they heard about Scoop and me chaperoning the china nest eggs.

"Haw! haw!" hooted Peg. "I didn't think the old man was smart enough to pull a trick like that."

Red was thinking of the tomato fight.

"I wish I had seen you squash Bid in the face."

"It was fun," I laughed.

"Bid'll probably lay it up against you and try to get even with you."

"I should worry. He started it."

"He's tricky."

"We can match his tricks with others."

Peg was still laughing over the china-egg trick.

"You wouldn't have thought it was so funny," I told him, "if you had been in our shoes. We were scared stiff, I want to tell you."

"Scared? What were you scared of?"

I told him about the man in the haymow, and about the pool of blood and the vanished egg.

"Gee!" cried Red, his eyes going big. "You sure had some wild night."

"I wish I had been there, Jerry," Peg spoke up. "I wouldn't have been scared like you. I would have found out who the man was and what he was doing there."

"We didn't know he was there," I further explained, "until he had escaped from the barn."

"You said you heard him when you were alone."

"I didn't say I heard him. As a matter of

fact I didn't hear a sound from him. I just had the sudden feeling that some one was watching me."

"Well," said Peg, "if it had been me, as I say, I would have done some speedy investigating."

"It's easy to talk," I grunted, kind of out of sorts with him in his brave talk. Still, I knew I had no reason to feel that way. For there isn't a braver kid in Tutter than Peg. That boy sure has grit. You can't scare *him*. I suspect that he would have gone into the haymow, as he said, if he had been in my place."

Pretty soon Scoop tumbled into the yard with a rolled-up newspaper in his hand. His eyes were dancing.

"Where's the egg?" he inquired eagerly.

"Over there by the oleander," I pointed.

He laughed.

"Bring it to the barn, Jerry. We're going to rejuvenate it."

I didn't know what he meant by that. Nor did Peg or Red, I imagine. But it sounded interesting. So I hooked the egg and we hurried to the barn.

"Scoop, the tailor," laughed Peg, when the leader brought out a measuring tape and began using it on the big egg.

Red gave a crazy yip.

"He's going to make Humpty-Dumpty a pair of panties."

"And a little coat and vest," I put in.

"Make him a pair of suspenders, too," laughed Peg.

But the measurer paid no attention to our nonsense.

"It's a bit oversize," said he presently, "but I guess we can get by with it."

"If it's too big," I laughed, "we can sandpaper it smaller."

He shook his head.

"No. An inch or two won't make any difference. For I imagine that some dodo birds laid bigger eggs than others."

"It's a goofle egg," I maintained in fun.

"No," he waggled, putting his tape away, "it's a dodo egg. I looked it up in Pa's encyclopedia."

"What's a dodo egg?" I inquired. "I never heard of such a thing."

"Why," he laughed, "a dodo egg is a dodo egg. *This* egg is a dodo egg. Sure thing. And it's worth a million dollars."

Peg looked at the leader as though he was something that the cat had dragged in.

"Cuckoo," he said, cranking up the side of his head.

"Yes, sir," Scoop went on, grinning, "it's a million-dollar egg, and nothing else but. I know what I'm talking about."

"Show me how to grab the million dollars," I said, "and you can have the egg."

He laughed and unrolled his newspaper.

"Read it for yourself," he said.

I did. And here is the article just as it appeared on the front page of the *Tutter Daily Globe*.

QUICK! PAGE THE SHADE OF P. T. BARNUM

YOU CAN BUY STOCK IN THIS EGG AND BECOME A MILLIONAIRE

From Chicago radio news sources comes the amazing tale of a "rejuvenated" dodo egg, alleged to have been recovered from King Tutankhamen's tomb, which is to be hatched in a modern incubator, in or near the Windy City.

Recently a Chicago newspaper editor was approached by the egg's "promoter," a middle-aged, roving-eyed man of restless personality, who glibly related the wonder tale, offering in conclusion to let the other in on what he contended was the greatest money-making scheme of the century.

So here is your chance to get rich. For the dispatch avers that "Dodo Stock" is available to the credulous. And, of course, the promoter's statement is not to be questioned that the hatched dodo bird, as an attraction, will easily net its exhibitors a million dollars.

A million-dollar egg! And some people of ordinary imagination thought that the "peak" price of eggs had been reached when Roy Chapman Andrews offered to sell a single dinosaur egg for five thousand dollars.

CHAPTER V

GETTING READY FOR OUR TRICK

RED'S eyes were big and round as he lifted them from the newspaper article and searched our faces.

"Can you imagine an egg worth a million dollars?" he cried. "Wough! I can hardly swallow it."

Peg hooted.

"Swallow what?—the egg?"

"No, the newspaper story."

Scoop gave a snort.

"Red, you're greener than I thought."

"Huh!"

"Don't you see the joke?"

"You're the only 'joke' I see."

"This promoter that the article tells about is a nut. He's got bats in his belfry."

"You mean he's cuckoo?"

"Sure thing."

"The newspaper doesn't say so."

"*Good* night! Can't you read between the lines? As though you could hatch an egg three thousand years old! The whole article is a joke."

Red hates to give in.

"I bet you," he argued, defiant-like, "that you can hatch a *regenerated* egg, no matter *how* old it is. Yes, sir-*ee!*"

"Regenerated!" yipped Scoop. "Say, kid, but you're good. You ought to have a medal. What do you use that makes you so bright?—Sapolio?"

"You've got the wrong word," I told the arguer. "It's rejuvenated, not regenerated."

"Of course," bluffed Red. "I know that. I said rejuvenated."

"Yes, you did, like so much mush."

"What does it mean?" put in Peg, who had been studying the newspaper. "I never heard the word before."

"I looked it up in the dictionary," said Scoop, "and the definition is, 'To make young and vigorous again.'"

There was a short silence.

"No one can do that to an egg," declared Peg, "no more than they can rejuvenate a dead cat and make it sing French."

"But if it isn't true," put in Red, who can be

an awful dumb-bell when he tries, "why did Mr. Stair publish it in his newspaper?"

"Because it's interesting," said Scoop, "and anything interesting is news."

I got in on the fun with a fake groan.

"And you told me my egg was worth a million dollars!"

"It is," grinned Scoop, "*if* you can hatch out a dodo bird."

"All I do is lose money," I groaned, gesturing despair. "Yesterday I lost five thousand dollars. And to-day I've lost a million dollars."

"You can *make* a million dollars," laughed Scoop, "if you'll do as I tell you."

"Maybe."

"All you've got to do, as I say, is to hatch out a dodo bird."

"Yah—that'll be easy—with a stone egg! What do I do?—set on it myself? Or do I hire a setting hen?"

"I was joking, of course. You couldn't hatch *this* egg in a hundred years. The point is that we're going to pretend that the egg is worth a million dollars."

"Like the dodo egg in the newspaper?"

"We're going to pretend that this *is* the dodo egg."

"And sell stock in it like the Chicago fellow?"

"Oh, no! That would be crooked. It would be taking money under false pretenses. And the law can put a fellow in jail for stuff like that. What we're after is fun. And we'll have our fun with the Cap'n."

"Hot dog!"

"He's been bragging to us how smart he is on this egg-hatching business. All right. We'll give him a chance to try out his wonderful incubator on the most valuable egg in the world."

Peg gave a doubtful laugh.

"It listens fine. But can we do it?"

"Of course we can."

"I doubt it. For the Cap'n is no dumb-bell. You know that. And when you start reciting this 'dodo' truck to him he'll tumble to your scheme and give you the horse laugh. He'll know you're trying to get back at him for the china-egg trick. In fact he'll be so suspicious of a trick that you won't be able to get within a mile of him."

Scoop pointed to the newspaper article.

"Will he be suspicious of a trick when he reads that?"

Peg felt himself slipping.

"Huh!" he grunted.

Scoop shoved the newspaper into his pocket.

"The dodo story," he continued, "is a streak of luck. Last night I lay awake for two hours trying to figure out how we could make a joke of the big stone egg. I couldn't get anywhere. But the dodo article makes everything easy. The Cap'n wouldn't believe *us,* as you say, Peg; but he'll believe the newspaper. And when the egg is shipped to him he'll think it's the real thing."

"But how can we ship the egg to him when it's already here?"

"We'll deliver it to the express company at Ashton. The Cap'n will think it was shipped to him from Chicago, for we're going to write him a letter, on a fake Chicago letterhead, letting on that we're a concern in the egg rejuvenating business."

"A fine scheme," Peg snorted. "First we go to Ashton to ship the egg; and then we go to Chicago to mail a letter. Where do we get the money for our railroad tickets?—or do we go by airplane?"

"We can hook a free ride to Ashton and back. It's only a few miles. As for the letter, that will be mailed at our post office. . . . You better grin, you old hardhead! . . . Hey, Red?"

"Yes, Mr. Rejuvenator?"

"Is your printing press in running order?"

"I guess so. I haven't used it for a coon's age."

"Well, tote it out and get it limbered up. For we've got to print our letterhead and get the letter into the post office this morning."

We had a lot of fun printing the letterhead and planning the letter. Scoop and I made up the stuff to be printed in the letterhead, looking up the big words in the dictionary, while Red and Peg set the type and fiddled with the printing press. Red had coaxed the treadle press out of his father by picturing how easily he could earn his spending money doing neighborhood printing. But his spelling was so bad no one would give him a repeat order. So there was very little printing done. Anyway, typesetting was too slow a game for Red Meyers. Speed is that boy's middle name.

Possibly you know what a letterhead is. All business firms have printed letterheads. Dad's brickyard letterhead reads:

THE TUTTER VITRIFIED BRICK
COMPANY
"Brick Makers Since 1884"
Tutter, Illinois.

Our letterhead was a big improvement over Dad's. We made it more interesting. Getting it printed, after a lot of mussing and fussing around, in which job Red got printers' ink all over his hands and face, as usual, Scoop and I hurried to his father's store, where we wrote the letter on a typewriter. We wanted the letter to be business-like. So that is why we wrote it on a machine. Here it is, letterhead and everything:

The Lazy Egg Shakes a Frisky Leg and the Sickly Egg Kisses the Undertaker Good-by When *Humpty-Dumpty* Comes into the Coop.

THE HUMPTY-DUMPTY EGG REJUVENATORS, INC.

Humpty-Dumptyize Your Eggs and Help the Poor Hens. For How Would *You* Like to be a Setting Hen and Work Faithfully for Twenty-one Days Without Knowing Whether It Was Going to be a Family or a Fizzle?

Humpty-Dumpty Building,
Chicago.

Cap'n Boaz Tinkertop, Incubator Expert,
Tutter, Illinois.
DEAR SIR:

We have heard about you and your wonderful incubator. In fact you have been pointed out to us as the smartest egg hatcher in the state of Illinois.

So we are sending to you, for hatching, a million-dollar dodo egg, taken out of King Tut's tomb and lately rejuvenated in our laboratories by our patented Humpty-Dumpty process.

We know that you will do a first-class hatching job.

When the dodo bird has been hatched, please write to us at our Chicago address. The man who will call for the young dodo bird will pay you for your work.

Also, we would like to have one of your cabinet photos to hang in our office, along with the pictures of other famous inventors, like Eli Whitney and Thomas A. Edison.

Respectfully,
JOHN HENRY HATCHER,
General Manager.

"That ought to do the business," grinned Scoop, as he sealed the letter in an addressed envelope.

Red and Peg overtook us on our way to the post office.

"This is our lucky day," laughed Peg. "For when I went down town to get a box to pack Humpty-Dumpty in, who should I run across but Pa, heading for Ashton to look up a lost paint shipment. I got him to take Humpty-Dumpty along."

"Did he ask you what was in the box?" Scoop inquired quickly.

Peg shook his head.

It was now within three quarters of an hour of Dad's train time. So I left the others at the post office and beat it for home.

Mother was in the front hall, with her back to the umbrella rack, fussing with a familiar traveling bag. She was too busy to notice me. So I tiptoed into the dining-room where Dad was talking loudly into the telephone.

"Dog-gone!" he scowled, jabbing the receiver onto its hook. "Higbee wants me to drive out to his clay pit." He jerked out his watch. "Maybe I can make it."

"Why don't you take Jerry along with you?" Mother suggested from the doorway. "He likes to drive the car. And he can drop you at the depot on the way home."

"Sure thing," I followed up eagerly.

Dad grinned at me.

"All right, Mr. Chauffeur. Come on."

Mr. Higbee is the man who gave me the red rubber boots for Christmas. He owns all the hills and hollows east of Name Rock bluff. He sells tons and tons of sand and clay. Dad uses the clay in his brickyard. The sand goes out of town. I've heard it said that the Higbees are very wealthy people. But you wouldn't think so to see the shabby house they live in. That's the way it is in this world: Some people with a little money make a big showing and other people with a lot of money sit back out of sight.

Bobby and Betty Higbee came running when Dad and I drove into the yard. They like me. I'm older, of course, and bigger. But they're good kids to play with. So I chased around with them until Dad came back to the car.

"There's just one thing I don't like about this brick manufacturing business," said he, grinning, when we were in the car.

"Yes?"

He slapped me on the knee where I've got the fishhook scar.

"It keeps me so blamed busy making and shipping bricks that I haven't any chance to get out and fool around with the best little pal in the world."

He meant me. You can see how he appreciates me.

"Are you still chumming with the Ellery boy?" he inquired after a moment.

I nodded.

"I chum with Peg and Red, too," I said.

"Um. . . . They're all pretty good kids, I think."

"We have lots of fun," I told him.

"I imagine so. And it's right that you should. For a boy is a boy only once in his life. But stick to the kind of fun that is wholly clean and manly. Mother and I expect it of you, Jerry."

"We went crystal hunting yesterday," I told him.

"Find any?"

I shook my head.

"And to-day——"

I stopped short. For Scoop had said that we were to keep mum about the dodo egg. But I quickly made up my mind to tell Dad about our joke on the Cap'n. For I have no secrets from him.

We were now in behind a big green truck. And suddenly I got hit in the face by an awful smell. Gee! It was worse than the time I was cornered by a skunk under Peg's hen house.

"Phew!" choked Dad, holding his nose.

It was the slaughter house truck, loaded with stuff for the rendering plant. Old bones and hunks of spoilt meat. In a jiffy I was holding my nose, too, and my lips were flattened tight together.

"It ought to make rich fertilizer," breathed Dad, when we had left the bad smell behind.

A few minutes later we drove into town. And when we drew up at the depot the train was coming around the bend.

"Good-by, Jerry, ol' pal! Take good care of Mother."

He was gone before I remembered I hadn't told him about the dodo egg.

CHAPTER VI

IN THE BARN

DIRECTLY after dinner we met at Scoop's store. We would use the eggs due the Cap'n, the leader said, as an excuse for our afternoon call on the old man. Otherwise, if we stumbled in on him just ahead of the Humpty-Dumpty letter, it might arouse his suspicions. Later on we would frame up some kind of an excuse to be on hand when the stone egg arrived by express, to help unpack it and get it properly into the incubator. By acting excited we would further deceive the tricked one and help the fun along.

"But we mustn't overdo it," cautioned Scoop, with a wise shake of his head. "For in the moment that he gets suspicious our joke is dead. For instance, when the letter is delivered this afternoon don't one of you immediately grab up last night's *Globe* and start yapping about the egg story on the front page. If anything, act sort of dumb. Let *him* do the leading."

"It won't be hard for Red to act dumb,"

laughed Peg. "All he has to do is to act natural."

"How about yourself?" flared up Red. "Who swam the creek to rescue Mrs. Camel's geese?"

"It wasn't me," denied Peg.

"Any old time it wasn't."

"Peg pulled *you* out of the creek one day," I reminded Red.

"Yah," hooted the big one. "You're the goose I rescued, Red. Haw! haw! haw!"

I turned to Scoop then.

"Are you going to tell the Cap'n about the man in his barn?"

"Not yet. I want to do some work in the barn first."

"Detective work?"

"Sure thing."

"I'm with you," I said.

"But there's no hurry about the detective work," he added. "We'll do that later on. It's more important right now to work our egg trick. Oh, boy! I bet we have fun."

Excited, high-pitched voices came to our ears when we turned into the Cap'n's yard.

The leader paused to listen and get his bearings.

"Evidently," he grinned, "the Tutter checker

champions are having a friendly afternoon game."

"It sounds like they're pulling noses," laughed Peg.

"Or kicking each other in the seat of the pants," I put in.

"Maybe old Caleb is pulling the Cap'n's peg-leg," added Peg.

"Come on," laughed Scoop. "Let's go in the house and see the fun."

The squabbling checker players were too busy glaring at each other across their checkerboard to notice us when we came into the room where they were.

"Git your sticky fingers offen my king," thundered the Cap'n.

"*Your* king!" screeched old Caleb Obed, a neighbor, glowering.

"Git your sticky fingers offen it, I tell you."

"I hain't goin' to set here like a dummy an' let you cheat me."

"Cheat you! *Me* cheat?"

"That's what you are—a great big cheat. You can't play fair, you can't."

"Why, you insultin' ol' he pirate!"

"That king of your'n never got to be a king reg'lar."

"Did, too."

"Didn't."

"Did, too, I tell you. I moved this 'un an' then this 'un an' you jumped this 'un——"

"Didn't," screeched old Caleb. "I jumped *this* 'un."

"No, sir!"

"Yes, I did. An' you know I did, you ol' cheat."

"Look here, Caleb Obed. Be you tryin' to insult me?"

"I'm only tellin' you what's true."

"Them's personal remarks—callin' me a cheat."

"If the shoe fits you kin put it on an' wear it, you kin. You *are* a cheat, so you be, an' you know it."

Here Scoop drew their attention.

"Good afternoon," he smiled, holding up the egg sack. "Here's some fresh eggs for you, Cap'n."

The players scowled at the interruption.

"Aigs?" muttered the Cap'n. Then he settled into his chair and grinned, cat-like. "Um. . . . Aigs, you say? Fresh aigs, hey?" and he gave a low, cackling laugh.

I guess you know what he was thinking about!

"Yesterday," said Scoop, sort of hanging his

head, repentant-like, which was a part of our scheme to make the other think we were licked, "I made a mistake and sold you six china eggs."

"Yes," drawled the Cap'n, slowly nodding his head, "I recall some sech mistake."

"It won't happen again," said Scoop, quiet-like, wanting the other to get the idea he was ashamed of himself for having had the nerve to try and put over a joke on some one older and smarter than himself.

The narrowed brown eyes sparkled with satisfaction.

"No? Well, they hain't no hard feelin's. The best of us make mistakes. Eh, Caleb?"

Down came the speaker's peg-leg with a fierce thump. And he bobbed out of his chair, his fighting eyes glued to the checkerboard.

"HEY!" he thundered. "Whar'd that king come from?" and he pointed with a jabbing, quivering finger.

No checker cheater ever looked more innocent than old Caleb.

"They warn't no king anchored thar a minute ago," roared the tricked one.

"Um . . ." purred old Caleb.

"You kin take it offen the board or I hain't a-goin' to finish the game."

A crafty light came into the cheater's eyes.

"A very good time fur you to quit. Yes, 'tis. Fur I've got you beat, anyway."

Up came the Cap'n's peg-leg under the checker-board. There was a shower of checkers.

"Heh! heh!" cackled old Caleb, rubbing his hands. "Had you beat, I did," and getting his hat he shuffled to the front door. "Some time when you kin play honest," he said, pausing stoop-shouldered in the doorway, "let me know an' I'll stop in an' we'll settle this matter of who is the best player."

The Cap'n watched his checker rival out of sight down the street, muttering and wagging his shaggy head.

"The ol' cheat!" he snorted.

"How about yourself?" came bluntly from Peg.

I knew why our big chum gave the old man that dig. Peg hates cheating. Most boys do.

But the Cap'n didn't catch on that the younger one was trying to shame him.

"Yes," he cackled, contented-like, acting as though he had been handed a bouquet, "I fooled him proper, I did. I got two kings over on him an' he only noticed one. Heh! heh! heh! Pretty smart, hey?"

Peg was disgusted. And getting my ear he whispered:

"I guess he needs to have a few tricks played on *him,* Jerry.

"He isn't any more of a cheat than old Caleb," I said.

The big one grunted.

"I don't see the fun of cheating in a game. What satisfaction is there in doing that, even if you win?"

"Old men are queer," I shrugged.

We stuck around, talking about this and that. And presently Red spotted the mail man.

"Some one's going to get a letter," he yipped.

The Cap'n took the letter from the mail man and squinted at the address, holding the envelope close to his big warty nose.

"Lemme git my glasses," he mumbled.

"Here they are," helped Scoop.

"Um. . . . It's a letter from Chicago. See the postmark? Must be from my Uncle Hank's b'y, who's workin' thar in Mr. Swift's slaughter house."

"I'll open it for you," offered Scoop, slitting the envelope with his finger. "There's your letter, Cap'n. Read it."

"Um. . . . 'Cap'n Boaz Tinkertop, Incubator Expert.' "

"That's you," said Scoop.

"Yes," the old man nodded, "that's me, all right. But the letter kain't be from my cousin, as I thought. It 'pears to be a business letter. See? It's all typewritten."

We crowded at his elbow, pretending a lot of curiosity.

" 'The Humpty-Dumpty Egg Rejuvenators, Inc.,' " read Scoop.

"Never heerd tell of sech a company," said the Cap'n.

"But they've heard of you," said Scoop. "See? It says so in the letter."

"Whar?"

"Right there in the first paragraph."

"Um . . ." purred the Incubator Expert, sort of swelling out. Then a wise look came into his face. "It's my incubator," he waggled. "I bet you they want to buy my invention."

"I shouldn't wonder," said Scoop. "For in the next paragraph it says something about a million dollars."

"WHAT?"

"Right there," Scoop pointed.

"Jumpin' Jupiter! Great balls of fire. *A million dollars!*"

"That's what it says."

"Man, oh, man!" cried Peg, thumping the incubator inventor on the back. "You're going to be rich. A million dollars! Think of it! You'll be able to buy the whole town."

"I—I never expected to git that much money out of my invention," fumbled the dazed old man, sweating.

Then he read the letter clear through.

"That's the closest I ever come to bein' a millionaire," he panted, swabbing his face and neck with a handkerchief.

"What's the matter, Cap'n?" inquired Scoop. "Aren't they going to buy your invention?"

"No."

"Gee! That's too bad."

"They jest want me to hatch a dodo aig for them."

"A which?"

"A dodo aig."

"What kind of an egg is that?"

"*I* don't know. The letter saiz the aig is bein' sent to me by express. Um. . . . Now, what in tarnation kind of a critter is a dodo aig? I thought I knew all about aigs. But, I swan, I never heerd tell of a dodo aig. No, sir, this 'dodo' business is all Greek to me."

"A dodo must be some kind of a hen," said Scoop.

"Dodo," mumbled the Cap'n, digging puzzled-like at his hair. Then his leathery face brightened. "Neow whar was it I seed somethin' 'bout a million-dollar dodo aig? Neow whar . . ." Dropping the letter he brushed us aside and pottered into the kitchen, returning with a newspaper. "Here 'tis," he cried. "On the front page."

Scoop let out his neck at the familiar newspaper article. "Sure enough," he waggled.

The fluttered egg hatcher shooed us toward the door.

"You b'ys better run hum. Fur I've got to study up in my 'cyclopedy what a dodo is an' plan heow best to go 'bout hatchin' it. An' heow kin a body plan things with a roomful of jabberin' kids? Git neow."

We held down our giggles until we came to Dad's clay shed. Then with the wooden wall between us and our victim we let loose.

"Oh! oh! oh!" roared Peg, holding his stomach. "This is a bigger joke than Cook discovering the north pole."

There was nothing more that we could do on our egg trick that day. So we doubled back to Zulutown, getting into the Cap'n's barn without its owner seeing us.

Peg and Red were curious to see the blood on the haymow floor. So up the ladder we went.

"It doesn't look like blood now," said Scoop, pointing to the blackened spot. "But it was sticky when we first discovered it last night."

"Maybe it's paint," laughed Peg.

"You poor fish! Paint doesn't dry that quick."

"It was blood," I told Peg. "There's no doubt about that."

We searched the floor for footprints. But there was none leading away from the bloody spot. This was disappointing.

Red suddenly let out a yip.

"Lookit!" he cried, fishing something out of the loose hay. "Here's your china egg."

Scoop and I stared at the recovered egg.

"Well, I'll be ding-fizzled!" cried the amazed leader. "What do you know about that!"

"Evidently," said Peg, working on the mystery with his mind, "your man stole the egg and then hid outside until you had gone. Then he came back and spent the night here."

Scoop looked dizzy.

"I can't understand it," he cried. "What is there about this egg that the man should take the trouble to steal it?"

"Let's break it open," suggested Red.

"It's nothing but a china nest egg."

"But let's make sure. Maybe it's got a diamond hid inside of it."

This was enough to wildly excite us. So we quickly smashed the egg. But there was nothing inside of it. As Scoop had said, it was just a common nest egg.

"The man hid the egg in the hay," waggled Peg, in further thought, "and that would mean that he intends to come back for it. Maybe he'll be back to-night. So, if we want to find out who he is, and what his game is, why not lay for him?"

"Hot dog!" cried Scoop, tickled with the plan.

Red was promptly worried.

"You aren't going to stay here to-night!"

"You tell 'em, kid."

"Aw! . . . I'd rather stay at home."

"And miss the fun?"

"Fun? What if the man should tackle us?"

"It's four of us to his one."

"Yes, but he may be four times bigger than we are."

"Don't be a calf, Red."

"I'd rather be a live calf," said Red, "than a dead hero."

I was disappointed in our further search of the barn. I had made myself believe that there was a secret here. But I could find no secret.

Finally we left the barn and went swimming. It was suppertime when we got home. And directly after supper we got our clubs and headed for Zulutown.

"Maybe we ought to get some tomatoes, too," laughed Scoop, when we came to the barn.

"Do you think that the Strickers will be back again to-night?"

"Maybe."

"I haven't seen them all day," I told him.

"Leave it to Bid to keep out of sight when you get the best of him. And we sure did clean up on him last night."

"I bet *he* did some 'cleaning up' when he got home," I laughed.

"Wasn't he a mess, though?"

Before the daylight was gone we went through the barn from top to bottom. There was no one there. Nothing had been disturbed since we had been there in the afternoon. To make a hiding place for ourselves in the haymow we piled the hay in one corner. It would cover us lightly; yet we would be able to see out.

"What if we get stepped on?" worried Red, when we were settled in our hiding place.

"That isn't liable to happen," said the leader. "But if it should happen we'll jump up and scare the man out of his wits."

"If he steps on me," shivered Red, "I'll die of heart failure."

"I hope he comes up here and goes to sleep," said Scoop. "For then it'll be a cinch to capture him."

"What are you going to do with him after you get him?"

"Find out his secret. And if it's an evil secret we'll turn him over to the law."

Well, it got dark after a while. And, as in the preceding night, I began to get shaky. I thought of what Red had said about the man being four times bigger than us. Maybe he was six times bigger, I thought.

Scoop had a flashlight.

"Nine o'clock," he told us, looking at his watch. Then he got up and tiptoed across the room to the haymow door. "I can see a light in the Cap'n's kitchen."

"Can you see the old man?" laughed Peg.

"No."

"He's probably in there studying his encyclopedia."

"To find out how to hatch a dodo bird?"

"Sure thing."

"He may not be as green as we think," I spoke up. "To-morrow when the egg comes he may fire it at us and kick us out."

Scoop got back under the hay.

"Gee!" he yawned, after a long silence. "This is kind of tiresome."

"What time is it now?" I inquired.

He flashed on the light and looked at his watch.

"A quarter of ten."

"How late are we going to stay?"

"Until the man comes."

"But suppose he doesn't come?"

"Then we'll stay all night."

I got sleepy after that. There was nothing for me to do. And figuring that I was safe with my three chums awake I shut my eyes and rambled off.

I don't know how long I slept. It may have been an hour; it may have been two or three hours. But suddenly I was awakened by a warm breath in my face. Some one was leaning over me! I could hear a heartbeat. Yes, and I could hear some one snoring, too, now that I was awake! It was Red or Peg or Scoop. I wondered, in a moment of wild fright, if my chums were all asleep.

"Scoop!" I screamed.

Instantly the hot breath left my face. Then I heard quick footfalls. The man was escaping.

"Scoop!" I screamed again, trying to find the leader in the darkness.

"Ho-hum!" came a sleepy voice. "Did you call me, Jerry?"

"Wake up!" I cried.

"Why! . . . What's the matter?"

"The man was here. He pulled the hay off my face. Then I felt his hot breath. *Listen!* He's going down the ladder."

The leader was wide awake now.

"Peg!" he called.

"Yes," came sleepily from our big chum.

"For the love of mud!" squeaked Scoop, and though I couldn't see him I could imagine that he was tearing his hair. "Have we *all* been asleep?"

"I thought you fellows were awake," I said.

"Yes, and *I* thought *you* were awake."

Getting out of the hay, we ran with our flashlight to the ladder. But we were too late. The man had gotten to the bottom of the ladder and had vanished into the night.

"Dog-gone!" cried Scoop, angry with himself and with every one else. "If we aren't the champion dumb-bells. . . . Where's Red?"

"Here I am," came a sleepy voice. "Is it time for breakfast?"

We told Red that the man had been in the haymow. And after that there was no sleeping for us. But everything was quiet in the barn until daybreak. The man didn't come back.

"He probably won't ever come back," growled Scoop, disgusted with the night's poor work. "For he knows we're wise to his hiding place now. And he'll keep away."

But that was once that the leader was wrong, as events proved.

CHAPTER VII

HUMPTY-DUMPTY ARRIVES

As I say, it was our plan to be on hand when the "dodo" egg was delivered by the express company. So we met at Scoop's store directly after breakfast. And as an excuse for our early-morning call at the Cap'n's house we carried a couple of fishing poles. But as you can imagine we had no intention of going fishing. The poles were just a blind.

We found the old man buzzing around his incubator, which had been carried from the barn into the kitchen.

"Hi, Cap," cried Peg, as we came into the house. "Better get your pole and come along with us."

"Heh?"

"Bullheads ought to bite good to-day. For it's cloudy."

"Kain't do it," the worker waggled.

"Pshaw!" grumbled Peg, acting disappointed. "What's the idea of staying at home when you can have fun fishing?"

"The dodo aig is comin' by express," fluttered the Cap'n. "An' I've gotta be here to receive it an' put it to hatchin'."

Scoop laughed.

"Did you find out what a dodo is?" he inquired.

"Yes. I looked it up in my 'cyclopedy. They hain't none now. They're extinct."

"So does a skunk," laughed Peg.

The old man straightened and scowled.

"So does a skunk what?"

"Stink."

"I didn't say 'stink,' you young smart Aleck. I said ex-*tinct*."

"Oh! . . ."

"What the Cap'n means," winked Scoop, "is that the dodo birds are all dead. Isn't that the dope?"

"Yes," the old man nodded. "When anything is *extinct* it's all gone; an' the dodo birds are all gone. Like the carrier pigeons. They've all been killed off."

"Then," said Peg, returning Scoop's wink, "if you hatch the rejuvenated dodo egg the dodo that you get out of the egg will be the only one in captivity. Hey?"

"Exactly. It'll be the only one in the world, *in* captivity or *out* of captivity. That's why the newspaper saiz it's worth a million dollars. Fur it kin go in shows. See? An' people will pay money to look at it."

"Do you get any stock in the dodo egg for hatching it?"

"No-o-o. The letter didn't say I would. They're goin' to pay me, the letter said."

"You ought to make them give you some stock in the egg," Peg waggled. "Two-three hundred shares. Then you'll get rich."

"The Cap'n doesn't need any dodo stock to get rich," I put in. "For he's got his incubator. He'll get a lot of money out of his invention."

This brought Scoop into the conversation again.

"Say, Cap'n, could you believe it that another inventor would burn up your incubator if he got a chance?"

The old man stopped his work under the unexpected question.

"Why, no," said he, looking puzzled. "What makes you ask that?"

"Do you know any inventors?"

"No."

"And you never heard that there was another man living near here who was working on an incubator like yours?"

"No."

"Have you seen any strangers hanging around here lately?"

"Um. . . . It seems to me I *did* see a stranger in my yard day before yesterday. Yes. He looked like a fureigner. Haid black hair an' a black mustache. I was a-goin' to ask him what he wanted, fur I took him to be a tramp. Then he dodged behind my barn an' I didn't see no more of him."

"Are you sure he didn't dodge *into* the barn?"

"Mebbe he did. I hain't sartin. But fur what reason be you askin' me all these questions?"

Scoop got my eye.

"Shall we tell him, Jerry?"

"Why not?" I said.

So we told the old man about the pool of blood in the haymow. A mysterious man had been hiding there, we said, and had later set fire to the barn by tipping the incubator over.

"We put the fire out," Scoop concluded, "and later the man came back and stole one of our china eggs. Can you think of any reason, Cap'n, why he should try to burn up your incubator, or your barn, and then steal and hide a common nest egg?"

The old man bent over his incubator.

"You b'ys better run 'long hum," he told us, acting as though he hadn't heard the question. "Fur I'm busy, as you kin see. An' I hain't in no mind to have you under my feet."

"We won't get in your way," promised Scoop. "We'll keep back."

"Git."

"Aw, Cap'n——"

"Git, I tell you."

Red grumbled when we were in the street.

"Shucks! We'll miss all the fun."

"Let's circle to the barn," suggested Scoop, "and watch from the haymow door."

"You didn't get much out of the Cap'n," I said to the leader, when we were in the barn. "If he knows anything about the pool of blood, he intends to keep the information to himself."

"He was too busy to talk to us."

"Maybe he didn't want to talk to us."

"Aw! . . ."

"Just the same," I waggled, suspicious of the old man, "we better keep a sharp eye on him. For he's crafty. You know that. Think of the tricks he's played on us! He may know more about this mysterious haymow gink than he's willing to admit."

Presently the express wagon came down the street.

"That's the box," whispered Peg, as the expressman disappeared into the kitchen through the east door.

Red pricked up his ears.

"I can hear the Cap'n pulling nails."

"Yah," chuckled Peg, "Humpty-Dumpty's being unpacked."

"The million-dollar dodo egg," I laughed.

"I hope the Cap'n's hammer doesn't slip," added Peg. "For it would be a calamity to have him crack the egg's shell."

"He'd be more liable to break his hammer," I said.

Scoop grinned.

"Don't be surprised," said he, "if Humpty-Dumpty comes flying through the screen door."

That, of course, is what would happen if the egg hatcher detected the fraud. For, as I have said before, the old man has an awful temper. When he gets mad he flies all to pieces.

And at the moment, in the thought of our possible detection, I made the quick decision that if the stone egg *did* come out through the door

I'd sort of brighten another corner of Tutter for a month or two. I'd keep away from Zulu-town—that was one sure thing.

But our luck was hitting on all cylinders. The Cap'n was completely deceived in the egg. And so I go on with the rest of my story.

CHAPTER VIII

THE REJUVENATION

EVENING came and the story of the million-dollar dodo egg was now on everybody's tongue. Such another wagging of heads over back-yard fences and porch railings I never hope to see. Usually people meeting in the street talk about the weather. But a more exciting topic of conversation to-night was Cap'n Tinkertop's million-dollar dodo egg.

A joke, of course—no one with common sense would believe such a ridiculous story. That is what the people said back and forth. But the funny part is that a good proportion of them *did* believe the story, notwithstanding. For people, it seems, are that way. A lot of them, I mean. They sort of *want* to believe the very things that they know are unbelievable. Take ghosts. We all know there is no such thing as a ghost. But how many people can go into a cemetery at night without shivering? Very few.

And so it was in this case. No one believed

"THAT'S THE BOX," WHISPERED PEG.

the story—so the people said. Yet everybody wondered if the egg would really hatch!

We got together that night after supper to talk over our successful egg joke and sort of pat ourselves on the back.

"Hot dog!" cried Scoop, stepping around in high feather. "We've got the whole town on its toes. There's more talk about our egg than there was about the future President last election."

"I never expected our trick to get such wide attention as this," said Peg.

"Nor me. But the Cap'n has been peddling the story of his wonderful egg all over Zulutown. That's how everybody happens to know about it."

"Isn't he the old dumb-bell! And it's nothing but a stone egg! Haw! haw! haw!"

"Sh-h-h-h!" cautioned Scoop. "Put the soft pedal on that 'stone egg' stuff. Some one may hear you."

"The old gent'll be mad enough to skin us alive when he learns the truth," put in Red.

"He had it coming to him," declared Scoop.

"I'll tell the world," I waggled, thinking of the kitchen-wrench joke. Boy, I'll never forget how I sweat that hot summer's afternoon as I trotted all over town on the fool's errand. It was nice to get even.

"I have a hunch," added Scoop, "that when the trick is exposed the Cap'n will let us alone and not bother us with any more of his tricks. And then, of course, if he does that we'll let him alone."

But Peg shook his head.

"That isn't the way it usually works out. One trick leads to another. And just as *you* fellows wanted to get even so will *he* want to get even. You wait and see if I ain't right."

"Any trick he can try," I laughed, "won't equal this trick. For, as Scoop says, we've got the whole town on our side."

"There's just one disappointing thing to me," said the leader.

"Yes?"

"I'm sorry we couldn't fool the Strickers, too."

"We could," I said, remembering Peg's suggestion, "if we had another big egg."

"Sure thing," laughed old hefty. "We could bury the second egg in a gravel pit, like I said."

Scoop danced around.

"Hot dog! That gives me an idea."

"It must be a peppy one."

"It is. Listen! We'll let the old man entertain the stone egg in his incubator for a few days. Then we'll swipe the egg. See? Everybody in town will be saying, 'Where did the million-dollar egg go to?' and 'Who stole the million-dollar egg?' There'll be a lot of excitement. All right. Here's my trick: We'll make a clay egg—the same size and everything. And we'll put a big fire-cracker in it. Then we'll let Bid find the egg. He'll think it's the million-dollar dodo egg. But before he gets his mitts on it we'll light the fuse. We can work it. *Bang!* Can't you imagine how his eyes'll stick out when the egg explodes? Oh, boy!"

We thought this was a pretty slick trick. And we said that we would make the clay egg the first thing in the morning, so that it would be nice and dry when the time came for us to use it.

I furnished the clay for the new egg and Scoop furnished the firecracker. However, he couldn't get a ten-incher. His pa sells fireworks, and there were some firecrackers put away in the store, but no big ones. So we had to use a three-incher.

We had fun making the clay egg. And putting it away in Red's barn to dry, we hurried into Zulutown to learn if anything new had happened there in the time that we had been busy.

We found ourselves in a stream of people. Every curious-minded man and woman in town was headed for Zulutown to see the wonder egg

—the famous million-dollar dodo egg. The Cap'n was excited in his sudden notoriety. And he made the people wait on his front porch while he shaved himself and polished the kitchen stove and got into his Sunday clothes. Then he opened his front door, nervously shaking hands with his visitors, with his necktie upside down. We were there along with the rest of the rubbernecks. And we went single file into the kitchen, past the incubator, where the big egg could be seen through the glass front, and out through the east door. Sort of funeral-like.

Mr. Stair was there. He's the man who owns the Tutter newspaper. You will remember him if you have read my third book, JERRY TODD AND THE OAK ISLAND TREASURE. He had a good laugh over the big egg. And he wrote down a lot of truck that the Cap'n told him. That evening there was a whole column of funny "dodo" news in the paper. The picture at the head of the column showed the Cap'n standing beside the incubator, pointing to the big egg with a pancake turner. And the south end of his Sunday necktie still pointed northwest.

Tutter is a small town. It is one of the smallest towns in La Salle County. And instead of murdering each other, as is frequently done in the big cities, if one is to believe the newspapers, the people, for the most part, go to church and lodge and otherwise behave themselves—which is all right, of course, and proper, but it's hard on the man who has to publish a daily newspaper.

So Mr. Stair was tickled pink in having the dodo egg to write about. And you can bet your Sunday shoes that he didn't spoil things by hinting around that the egg was a hoax. No, sir-ee! So far as his printed opinion was given the egg was the real stuff. And great historical fame was ahead for Tutter, he declared. For future generations would learn that our town was the birthplace of the world's only surviving dodo bird.

As I say, Dad is forever up to some kind of nonsense or other. And what do you know if he didn't send me a Christmas card! In the middle of summer! That's Dad, for you. I bet he hunted an hour to find that particular card, for, as you know, Christmas cards aren't usually on sale in July. He wrote under the Christmas tree that the snow was seventeen feet deep in Indianapolis and it was a big inconvenience for him not to have his overcoat along. He was coming home Sunday, he said, if the train could buck the snow-drifts. I was glad to know that he would be home so soon. For I was eager to tell him about our successful egg joke. He knew how the Cap'n had tricked me in the kitchen-wrench joke. And he would be glad to know that I had gotten even with the old man in such a clever way. More than being glad with me, he would tell me that I was pretty smart.

I met him at the depot. He was tickled to see me, as I knew he would be, and let me carry his traveling bag. On the way through town he treated me to a banana split.

But he didn't laugh, as I had thought he would, when I told him about the dodo egg. He said, in a grave way, that it was all wrong for boys to play tricks on an old man. And four against one was unfair.

Well, I tried to be stubborn in my defense. You know how it is with a boy in a moment like that. He hates to be cornered and have to own up. But I didn't succeed very well in my stubbornness. For Dad was right. I could see it now. I just hadn't thought about it before. I had been too busy patting myself on the back.

"Your scheme is clever," he said, sort of quiet-like, as though he wanted to set me right in as friendly a way as possible, "but it's tricky. Take the Humpty-Dumpty letter. It's a sort of lie all the way through. For you aren't a concern in the egg rejuvenating business. Nor did the egg come out of King Tut's tomb."

"*He* fooled us," I cried.

"True enough. And your desire to get even is perfectly natural. But I wish you had passed up the temptation with a grin. For, as I say, he's an old man, and your friend. He truthfully thinks he's an authority on egg hatching. And I hate to think of his humiliation when he learns, as he must, that the egg is a hoax and that he is a neighborhood laughingstock."

I felt miserable.

"I wish I hadn't done it," I confessed.

Yes, I was good and ashamed. For I saw what I had done. I don't like to hurt people. And I wanted to go to the Cap'n now and square myself.

But there were my chums. If I went back on them they would turn me down. I didn't like to think of that. For Scoop and Red and Peg mean a lot to me. I wondered if I could make them see our mistake. I hoped I could. For I didn't want to lose their friendship.

You can see what a fix I was in. And the disgusting part is that an old slaughter house truck was the cause of it all. Absolutely! For if

Dad and I hadn't got tangled up in the green truck's bad smell that Tuesday morning I would have told him about our intended egg trick. Then he could have stopped me in time. It's tough on a fellow to have his luck turned upside down by a stinking old bone truck. I'll tell the world!

It came Monday morning, and I was helping Mother with the washing when the Cap'n called me up on the telephone.

"Jerry," he began, sort of whining-like, "kin I git you to come over an' help me fur a spell? The dodo aig needs attention, an' the incubator lamp needs fillin', an' I've got a' awful pain in my right laig. It's jest like gittin' butcher knives shoved into me every time I step on it. Thar comes the pain neow! Oh-h-h-h-h!"

I explained to him that I was running the electric wringer for Mother and couldn't leave the house until the washing was done.

"But Red's out back," I added quickly. "I'll send him."

I was glad that the Cap'n had sent for me. It would make it easier for me to square myself with him. And as soon as I could get away I started briskly for Zulutown. On the way I met Peg and Scoop. The latter had a sack of gumdrops. They gave me some of the candy. And it was then that I told them that I was going to do the right thing by the Cap'n in the way of telling him the truth about the stone egg and apologizing to him.

Scoop laughed.

"You make a lot of needless grief for yourself, Jerry. Didn't I say we were going to swipe the stone egg in a day or two? And what did we make the firecracker egg for?"

"To fool the Strickers."

"Of course. And if we swipe the Cap'n's egg that'll leave him out, won't it? If we keep mum no one but ourselves will ever know the truth about the egg. Does that satisfy you?"

Here the fourth member of our gang came up on the run.

"Humpty-Dumpty!" he panted, falling on us.

When Red gets excited you can tell it at a glance. For it sticks out all over his freckled face like bumps on a squash. And just now the most noticeable scenery on the front side of his head was a pair of bulging eyes and a big hole in the section where he usually keeps his mouth.

Scoop laughed and tossed a gumdrop into his mouth.

"What's the matter, Red? Did the Incubator

Expert heave Humpty-Dumpty at you through the kitchen door?"

"Humpty's comin' to life!" gasped Red.

Scoop gave a crazy yip.

"Impossible!" he jeered, acting silly. "For the *Mother Goose* book says, 'All the King's horses and all the King's men couldn't put Humpty-Dumpty together again.' There you are. You can't argue against that."

Red was rattled. In his excitement he didn't know which end he was standing on.

"It's so," he screeched, jumping up and down. "It's so, I tell you. The egg is *hatching.* I heard it. So did the Cap'n. He's got one of these ear-listener things—a doctor's stethoscope, or whatever you call it—you know what I mean—and when I put it on the egg I could hear a heartbeat. Just as plain as anything. The Cap'n says it's the dodo getting ready to come out of its shell."

"Shell your granny!" exploded Peg. "That egg hasn't got any more of a shell than a grindstone. That's what it is—a stone, and nothing else but."

"We thought it was a stone," fumbled Red, digging crazy-like at his hair.

"It *is* a stone."

"It can't be. For it's hatching, I tell you. I heard it. It must be a real dodo egg."

This put Scoop and Peg into full flight for Zulutown. Red took after them. I tried to do the same. For I was crazy to see the hatching egg. But I couldn't run. My legs were wabbly. I could scarcely stand. I didn't know what was the matter with me at first. Then I realized that the shock of learning all in an instant that I was a millionaire was almost too much for me.

Of course, to get down to fine facts, I wasn't a millionaire yet. But I would be a millionaire as soon as the dodo got a hole punched through its shell. For the egg was mine. I could lay claim to it as its finder. And owning it, certainly whatever came out of it was mine.

The thought of owning a million dollars all in one hunk put me dizzy as well as loose-kneed. I'd buy an automobile and a motor boat and a shotgun and a pair of fishing boots and a new bicycle and an ice-cream factory. I'd buy a candy factory, too, and a gum factory. Oh, I'd buy all kinds of factories—a baseball factory and a toy factory and every other kind of a factory that manufactured things that I liked. I'd buy *everything*.

And with so much money in my pocket I could

easy enough square myself with the Cap'n. I thought of that. And it was a good thought, too.

"Jerry Todd!" came a sharp voice. "What *is* the matter with you? Be you out of your senses, child?"

Instead of starting a long conversation with talkative old Mrs. Higgins I gravely held out my hand and let her shake it. She would brag about it afterwards, when I got to be a millionaire. But that was all right with me. I'm not stuck-up or selfish.

Then in the recovered use of my legs I lit out for Zulutown.

CHAPTER IX

THE PURRING EGG

JUST imagine how excited you'd be to have a wizard come along with his magic wand and jiggle it at you and change you in magic from a street kid into a king. Like in the book called the *Arabian Nights.*

That's the way it was with me, sort of. One minute I was a poor boy, with a worry in my mind. The next minute I was a care-free millionaire.

Maybe if I had been less excited over my sudden good fortune I would have tried to figure out how it had happened. For a number of things needed explaining.

But all I could think about was the million dollars itself and the fun it would bring me. Oh, boy, wasn't I lucky! I walked on air, as the saying is, in the thought of my good fortune.

Then I became ashamed of myself. I was acting piggy. Yes, I was. For how about Scoop and Red and Peg? They were my pals. And I had given not a particle of thought to sharing my fortune with them, as a loyal chum should.

So to do the right thing by my pals I decided to give each of them ten thousand dollars. Then I raised the amount to twenty-five thousand dollars. But even this big amount of money seemed pretty small as compared to my nine hundred and twenty-five thousand dollars. So I generously jumped it to fifty thousand dollars apiece. That shows you how good-hearted I am.

Putting on extra speed, I tried to overtake the others to tell them of my generous decision. But they had too much of a start on me. And when I tumbled into Cap'n Tinkertop's east door several minutes later Scoop already had the stethoscope hanging in his ears.

"It's so, Jerry," he shouted at me. "The egg's hatching. I can hear it."

I took the stethoscope in turn and bent over the big egg. And sure enough I could hear a distinct heartbeat. In the exciting moment all I could think of was a walking barrel of money thump-thump-thumping on my front door to be let in.

Talk about Fortune knocking once on every fellow's door! Bu-lieve me this was *some* fortune that had come to live with me.

Cap'n Tinkertop was fidgety and cross until we had closed the incubator.

"Neow keep 'way from it," he ordered sharply, from his pillowed chair in the front-room doorway. "Fur if you don't the dodo is liable to git chilled in its shell. I hain't a-wantin' *that* to happen. An' I hain't a-goin' to let it happen, nuther. So the less you kids hang 'round here to bother the better it'll suit me."

"Aw, let us stay and help you," begged Scoop.

"Jerry's goin' to stay. I ast him first. An' one's enough."

Scoop scowled as he kicked open the screen door. He always likes to be the head push in everything. That's his nature. And he was mad now because I was the lucky one. I felt pretty big. But I tried not to let on.

Under the Cap'n's directions I filled the incubator lamp and trimmed the wick. Then he put me to sweeping. This was hard work. My arms got tired and my nose got clogged up. But I didn't lay down on the job.

"Neow," said the invalid, who was taking it easy in his soft chair, "you kin start in an' dust."

This took another half hour of hard work.

"When do we eat?" I inquired, parking the dust cloth on its hook by the pantry door.

"Well," drawled the old man, "that's up to you. They's pertaties in a sack on the pantry floor, an' aigs, an' a hunk of ham. An' they's some canned stuff an' a pail of honey high up on the shelves. You kin jest pick out what you want. An' whatever suits you suits me."

I didn't try to cook anything fancy. Just plain truck like boiled potatoes and fried ham and eggs and coffee.

"I never had a better meal in all my life," bragged the Cap'n, wiping the catchup off his necktie. Then he picked at a clogged tooth with his fork. "Everything cooked jest right. Even to the coffee. Neow they hain't one person in a hundred kin bile coffee the way I like it. But *this* coffee . . ." He leaned forward, his chin whiskers thrust out. "Be they any more in the pot, Jerry?"

I fished a bug out of the pot and gave him what was left of the coffee.

"Um. . . . This is what *I* call real coffee."

I felt good in his praise.

"If you want me to," I offered, swatting a fly in the butter, "I'll stay and cook supper for you. And we'll have hot biscuits and honey."

The brown eyes warmed up.

"Um. . . . I 'preciate what you're doin' fur

me, Jerry. Yes, sir, you're a good b'y. An' you kin bake fine biscuits. But I hate to be takin' up all your time."

I wanted to be close to the hatching egg. And that is why I was so eager to wait on him.

"My time isn't very valuable," I said quickly. "And I can stay and help you just as well as not."

"Well, I calc'late you kin stay an' make supper fur me if that's the way you feel about it. Fur it's a fact I would like to have hot biscuits an' honey to-night. An', of course, if you don't bake 'em fur me they won't be baked, fur, as you kin see, I kain't move out of my chair to wait on myself. My poor laig! Oh-h-h-h-h! Every time I move it it perty near kills me."

In the next hour I washed a million dishes and frying pans. For the pantry and kitchen cupboard were cluttered with dirty dishes of all kinds. I could almost imagine that the Cap'n had been saving them up for me. I can't say that I like dish washing. It's a girl's job. So as you can imagine I wasn't a bit sorry when the last clean dish went into the cupboard.

The Cap'n sort of beamed at me as I dropped into a chair to rest my legs.

"I jest feel 'shamed of myself lettin' you do all the work," said he, warm-like. "An' neow that you've got the dishes done I hain't a-goin' to ask you to polish the stove. No, sir, you've done enough fur one day. So you jest set right whar you be an' rest. The stove needs polishin' awful bad, as you kin see, after me lettin' the oatmeal bile over on it this mornin'. But we'll jest let it go till some day when I'm able to be 'round. Anyway, I hain't sure I've got enough blackin' to go all over it. Jest look on the top shelf in the pantry, Jerry. . . . Find it? Yes, that's it. Shake it up good before you put it on. That's the way."

I began to think all of a sudden that the old man was working me. It looked that way. For no sooner had I finished one job than another was shoved at me. But in my own interests I set to work on the hot stove. For, as I say, I wanted to be near the hatching egg. And I encouraged myself in the thought of the great good fortune that lay ahead of me. What was a little work like this, I told myself, when the reward was a million dollars!

In the time that I was sweating in the nasty stove-polishing job, with my face and hands daubed up, Scoop came quietly to the side porch and flagged my attention by rolling pebbles across the porch floor. Then he wrote something on the stone step and disappeared.

The Cap'n was now fast asleep in his easy chair. This was a good thing for me, I told myself in sudden satisfaction. And anxious to know what my chum was up to I dropped the polishing cloth and hurried quietly to the door.

Chalked on the step was an arrow, pointing south, and the word "barn."

For the past two or three days we had given no particular thought to the barn mystery. Having scared the man away we were all of the opinion that he would stay away. More than that, we figured that he had left town. So accordingly we had given up the mystery as something out of our reach.

But now I was instantly excited again in the thought that Scoop had gotten track of the man. Either that or he had uncovered some new part of the mystery in the barn. I was all prepared to see another pool of blood, or even to meet the man himself. But in this I was disappointed. For what Scoop wanted to see me about was the hatching egg.

"Well, Jerry," he grinned, when I had joined him in the barn, "how's Humpty-Dumpty?"

"Still purring," I told him.

I could tell by his actions that he had been doing some deep thinking.

"Jerry," he waggled, "there's a mystery about this egg of ours."

I thought it wasn't any too early in the egg's hatching to let him know whose egg it was. Then there would be no misunderstanding, or disappointment on his part, or on the part of Red or Peg, later on.

"You don't mean *our* egg," I corrected. "You mean *my* egg. It was me, you know, who found it."

"We sure were fooled proper," he went on, entirely missing the point of my remark. "We thought it was a stone. And now it turns out to be a real egg."

"I said at the time that it was an egg,"I reminded. "But you fellows wouldn't listen to me. You knew it all."

"It looked liked a stone. And it was heavy like a stone." He shook his head. "I can't understand it."

"Can't understand what?"

"How we could have been so completely fooled. It makes me feel cheap."

"*I* don't feel cheap," I said, thinking of my coming fortune.

"Huh?"

"I'm going to be rich," I bragged to him. Then I added quickly: "So are you and Red and Peg. For I'm going to give each of you fifty thousand dollars."

He laughed.

"Don't count your chickens before they're hatched, Jerry."

"This isn't a chicken," I corrected.

"Well, then, don't count your dodo before it's hatched."

"I'm not worrying. For it sure has a healthy purr."

He knit his forehead.

"I guess it's a real dodo egg, all right. I won't argue that. But I can't figure out how it came to be in the cave. That's a queer thing."

"Maybe Mrs. Dodo likes caves," I grinned. "And that is why she built her nest in one."

"You poor fish!"

"The day we robbed the nest," I added in more nonsense, "she was out calling on her neighbors. Or maybe she was gathering acorns for winter."

"Pa's encyclopedia says that the dodo birds are

all dead. Besides, there never was a dodo in this country. The dodo country is over near Africa."

"Well, what of that?"

"I'm trying to make you understand that the egg wasn't laid in the cave by a dodo hen."

"Who laid it?—a dodo rooster?"

"Some man."

I gave a yip.

"He must be *some* man, all right, to lay an egg. For that's more than you can do. And think what a wonderful guy *you* are!"

"Oh, I didn't mean that," he said quickly. "I meant he *put* the egg in the cave with his hands."

At the moment I thought of the newspaper article.

"Do you suppose," I said, more serious now, "that there's a possible connection between our egg and the Chicago egg?"

"Peg says it's the same egg."

"But how does *he* know?"

"Oh, he's guessing, of course. He hasn't any proof. Still, I believe he has the right dope. For there hardly can be two rejuvenated dodo eggs around here. But for the life of me I can't figure out *why* the egg was brought here from Chicago and put in the cave. That's a puzzler. It wasn't hid. Nor was it in any way protected."

"You'll begin to believe me after a while," I waggled.

"What do you mean?"

"*I* think that there's a real dodo hen strutting around here."

"Aw, shucks! Come down to earth."

"Maybe it escaped from a circus."

"But there aren't any, Jerry."

"Aren't any what?—circuses?"

"There aren't any living dodo hens. They're all dead."

"All but one."

He threw up his hands in disgust.

"Aw, there's no use talking to you!"

I grinned. For it's fun to get his goat.

"All right," I said. "What is it you want me to believe?"

"Peg says, and I back him up, that this is the Chicago egg. But, as I say, I can't understand why it was put in the cave. It's worth a pile of money. Yet it was left unprotected."

"It's hard shell was protection for it."

"Yes. But if you owned a million-dollar egg——"

"I do own one," I cut in, to the point.

"——if you owned a million-dollar egg," he went on, "would you leave it in a cave in plain sight to be picked up and lugged off, or possibly kicked to pieces, by any Tom, Dick or Harry who happened to come along?"

"No, sir-ee," I waggled. "I'd put *my* million-dollar egg into Cap'n Tinkertop's incubator."

I figured that would sink in. But it didn't.

"Peg is all worked up over the mystery," the other went on. "He has the idea that the man who put the egg in the cave is likely to be hanging around—sort of trying to solve the mystery of its disappearance. So he's gone up the railroad track to the ravine."

"To watch the cave?"

"Sure thing."

I was suddenly troubled in the thought that I might have to give up the egg to its earlier owner.

"Not on your life," Scoop waggled, when I had told him my thoughts. "We found the egg; and we're going to keep it."

"*I* found it," I corrected again, getting out of patience with him. He sure was dumb. Couldn't he take a hint, I wondered. I was going to be generous with him and give him fifty thousand dollars, as I had told him. But, bu-lieve me, he could lay off the million dollars. *That* was mine.

"And there's another thing, Jerry," he went on.

"Yes?"

"Plainly there *is* such a thing as egg rejuvenation, though we made a joke of it in our Humpty-Dumpty letterhead."

"I'd like to know the secret," I said.

"We'd have a fortune in our grasp if we did know the secret."

I twisted my mind around and got an idea.

"Maybe the rejuvenation was done in the cave," I suggested. "You've been wondering why the egg was put there. Maybe that explains it."

The other stared at me.

"Why, I hadn't thought of that. But I bet you're right."

"I'm always right," I grinned, "except when I'm wrong."

"And that would explain why the egg was left exposed, too," he ran on in growing excitement.

"Sure thing," I nodded, proud of myself in my smartness.

"It was dipped in the rejuvenator stuff——"

"Or painted with it," I put in.

"——and left in the cave to dry."

"Exactly. And when the rejuvenator came back to get his rejuvenated egg," I grinned, "it had dried up so completely that he couldn't find it."

"But why was it necessary to bring the egg to

Tutter to rejuvenate it?" was Scoop's next thought. "And why was the rejuvenating done in a cave?"

I threw up my hands.

"Yank your steering wheel," I told him. "You're going around in a circle."

A grin jumped into his face.

"Jerry, there's a real mystery here. There's no doubt about that. And you can trade me off for eight cents' worth of ripe dog meat if we don't have a barrel of fun in our detecting."

"I hope we don't lose the egg," I said.

"No chance, kid. We're too smart."

"The rejuvenator gink may find out where it is and get busy."

"We'll outwit him if he tries to snitch it on us."

Here Peg tumbled into the barn all out of breath.

"I saw him, fellows!" the newcomer cried.

"Saw who?" inquired Scoop, excited. "The rejuvenator?"

Peg pumped his head.

"He's a humpback. I saw him come up the ravine from the railroad track. Sort of skulking along in the bushes. And when he dodged into the cave I beat it for here to tell you about it."

"A humpback!" cried Scoop. He thought of

the only humpbacked man in Tutter. "Was it Matsy Bacon?"

Peg shook his head. And there was a queer look in his face now.

"Fellows, I've got a surprise for you."

We stared at the big one, wondering what was coming.

"You know the man in the haymow. Well, I've got a hunch I know who he is."

"Who?" cried Scoop.

"The humpback."

"What makes you think that?"

"You know what the Cap'n told us. He said a strange man was hanging around here last Monday."

"A foreigner," supplied Scoop, "with black hair and a black mustache."

"Exactly," waggled Peg. "And that description fits my man to perfection."

"Evidently," I put in, thinking, "the man was hanging around here *before* we brought the egg here."

"Sure thing. He was sleeping in the barn. But I guess he's hiding in the ravine now."

Scoop was puzzled.

"Do you suppose he's still searching in the ravine for the egg?"

"It looks so."

"He must be dumb not to know where it is. For everybody else around here knows where it is."

"Maybe we ought to hide it," I put in.

"Yes," agreed Scoop, "we've got to do something to save it." Then he laughed at thought of a sudden scheme. "How about abducting it?"

"What do you mean?" I cried.

Still laughing, the leader recited his scheme.

"Hot dog!" I cried, excited in the fun that was coming. Then, to make sure that the scheme would work, I scooted into the kitchen and measured the incubator and the trap-door into the cellar.

"At ten o'clock," said Scoop, when we separated, in agreement that we would meet at the Cap'n's house that night and commit the crime.

"At ten o'clock," said Peg, heavy-like.

CHAPTER X

ABDUCTING HUMPTY-DUMPTY

DONG! . . . Dong! . . . Dong! . . . Dong! . . . Dong! . . . Dong! . . . Dong! . . . Dong! . . . Dong! . . . Dong!

I sort of shivered as the tenth stroke of the tower clock on College Hill boomed metallic-like on the night air and died away in the distance. For the hour was come to commit the crime. And it makes a fellow nervous to tackle a job like that without a little practice.

The other fellows had counted the strokes of the tower clock, too. And now a voice came over the top of Cap'n Tinkertop's ash pile.

"I—I wish I was home," quavered Red Meyers. "I—I don't like this abducting business."

"It's fun," giggled Peg.

"Fun! How do you get that way?"

"Of course it's fun," put in Scoop. "It's something new. You've heard of people being abducted. But this is the first time an egg was ever abducted."

"*You* may think it's fun," grumbled Red. "But I wish I was out of it."

There was a sound back of us.

"Oh! . . ." gurgled the nervous one. "What was that?"

"What was what?"

"I heard something. Over there by the barn. Maybe it was the humpback."

"All I heard was a rat," I told him.

Peg snickered.

"Don't be too sure it was a rat, Jerry. It wouldn't surprise me if it was a ghost. For one time a man hung himself in that barn."

Red gurgled again.

"For the love of mud," laughed Scoop, giving Peg a shove, "don't scare the kid to death. Come out of it, Red."

"I wish I was home."

The leader got ready for business.

"Who's got the rope?" he inquired.

"Me," said Peg.

"Hang onto it. For we'll need it in a few minutes."

There was a scuffle of feet in the darkness.

"If we get put in jail for this," shivered Red, "I'm going to lay the blame on you, Scoop Ellery. For you coaxed me into it."

"They can't put a fellow in jail for hiding his own egg."

"But the Cap'n can make it hot for us for breaking into his house."

"We aren't *breaking* into his house. Jerry left the kitchen window unlatched. All we've got to do is to raise the window and *crawl* in. That isn't *breaking* in. Not by a long shot."

"It's just the same as breaking in, *I* bet. You wait and see what the law says."

"The law your granny! We're safe. For hasn't the Cap'n told us time and again that we could go into his house whenever we wanted to?"

"Yes, but this is different."

"I suppose we dassn't touch our own egg, hey, just because it happens to be in some one else's incubator."

"We have no right to steal the incubator."

"Putting it in the cellar isn't stealing it."

"Of course not," backed up Peg, who was eager to go ahead in the leader's scheme. "It isn't stealing unless we take it away."

We were now on the side porch. And the leader hissed for silence.

"Hear anything of the old man?" breathed Peg, when Scoop put his ear to the door.

"No."

"He usually snores."

"I can't hear him."

"Of course, you can't," I spoke up. "For I closed his bedroom door."

"Good work, Jerry," the leader bragged on me. "Who's got the flashlights?"

Peg and I spoke up.

"Fine! Now, fellows, let's make it snappy. But, for Pete's sake, don't fumble. Watch your steps. For if you bump into a chair, or make a noise, we're liable to get the Cap'n out of bed. Remember, it's a million dollars in our pocket if we succeed."

The nerve of him, I thought. A million dollars in *our* pocket!

Raising the window, the leader went noiselessly over the sill, disappearing into the black well beyond. Peg and I followed.

"Go-osh, it's dark!" chattered Red, the last one through the window.

Suddenly there was a crash.

"Good night!" squeaked Scoop.

"I—I fell," whined Red.

"I thought the house fell."

"I skinned my knee. Oh-h-h-h!"

"Shut up! Don't you realize we've got to be

quiet? What do you think this is?—a football game?"

Bang! went a chair.

"Throw him out," growled Peg.

"I—I couldn't help it," whined Red. "I can't see in the dark."

"Then take this flashlight," I offered.

Scoop was almost in despair.

"Listen, Red. We've got to be quiet, I tell you. For we've got a job here. And the Cap'n isn't deaf."

"What do we do first?" Peg wanted to know.

The leader got down to business.

"Help me tie the rope around the incubator. Turn your flashlight, Red—there isn't anything over there in that corner except a pair of old boots! That's it. Jerry, you go down cellar and steady the incubator as we lower it through the trap-door. Have you got it tied, Peg? Fine! Here we go."

I can't say that I was tickled over the cellar job. For I knew what a deep, dark hole it was. But I didn't crawfish. I wasn't going to act like Red. The big calf! And raising the trap-door in the floor, I went cautiously down the ladder, throwing the light ahead of me to scare the sewer rats into their hole. You can bet your Sunday shirt I didn't want to step on one!

The air was clammy-like. It made me think of dead people. And I gave a gurgling screech when a dangling spider brushed the back of my neck.

"Who put a nickel in you?" hissed Peg through the trap-door.

"It was a spider," I shivered.

"We thought you were practicing for a concert."

"*You* aren't funny," I growled.

Down came the wooden incubator inch by inch.

"Can you handle it, Jerry?"

"Easy," I hissed back.

I thought I could. But even as I spoke something went wrong with the rope. And before I fully realized my own or Humpty-Dumpty's danger the incubator fell with a crash, pinning me to the dirt floor.

There was a cry from above. Then in a clatter of feet Scoop and the others tumbled down the ladder to see who was hurt the worst, me or Humpty. Of course they hoped it was me.

They finally got the incubator off my neck. I wasn't hurt much. Nor was Humpty-Dumpty, we learned. But I want to tell you my heart was in my mouth when we opened the incubator door. For I expected nothing else than to see the soft part of Humpty's million-dollar gizzard oozing out through a crack in the shell.

Scoop wiped the sweat from his forehead and started breathing again.

"Gee-miny crickets, that was a narrow escape!"

"I'll tell the world," I gasped.

"It was a good thing you were on the bottom, Jerry."

"Yah," laughed Peg, "you made a nice soft cushion."

Red put the big egg to his ear.

"I can't hear a thing," he told us.

Scoop laughed.

"Of course you can't—not without the stethoscope. I found that out yesterday."

Wanting to make sure that Humpty was still breathing and was inwardly none the worse for his fall, I offered to get the stethoscope, which hung on the pantry doorknob.

"Make it snappy," said Scoop, when I started up the ladder. "For we want to put a quick finish on this job and get out of here."

In the time that we had been in the cellar the

moon had climbed over a bank of clouds and I could now glide about the kitchen without the aid of my flashlight.

But before returning to the cellar with the stethoscope I tiptoed to the Cap'n's closed bedroom door and listened. For it had occurred to me that he might be astir, having heard the commotion, particularly the crash of the incubator to the cellar floor.

But the bedroom was a well of silence.

Thus assured that we would be able to complete our job and escape from the house undetected, I scrambled down the ladder, handing the stethoscope to Scoop, who promptly bent over the egg.

"Still purring," he told us, spreading his mouth in a happy grin.

Sure enough I could hear the egg's even heartbeats when I put the stethoscope to my ears. "Money! Money! Money!" is what it seemed to say. "Money! Money! Money!"

Oh, how rich I was going to be! I thrilled at the thought of it.

"Well," said Scoop, "I can see no further need of staying here. So let's move. . . . Ough! What was that?"

"A rat," I told him. "They come in through

the sewer," I explained, pointing to a tile in the foundation.

He shrugged.

"I don't blame the Cap'n for wanting to sidetrack this hole. For that rat was big enough to chaw the carburetor out of his wooden leg."

"He quit using the cellar on account of the ladder," I explained. "For, with his peg-leg, it was hard work climbing up and down."

"I can imagine so. Well, let's hope he continues to keep out of here until Humpty is ready for market."

I mentioned the invalid's lame leg.

"Even if he wanted to come down here," I said, "he couldn't."

"That's so," waggled Scoop.

Red started growling again in his usual cheerful way.

"It's a crazy scheme, I tell you. And it'll get us into law trouble just as sure as shootin'. You mark my word. For as soon as the Cap'n finds out that his incubator has been stolen he'll telephone to Bill Hadley, the town marshal. And this is the first place they'll look."

But the leader couldn't see it that way.

"Oh, no," he laughed, in confidence in his scheme. "Bill is too good a policeman to try and find the missing incubator so *easy*like. He'll want to use his detective science, or whatever you call it. I know Bill! And it doesn't take any detective science to lift a trap-door and say, 'Here it is!' I tell you, Red, the incubator's safer here than it would be any other place in the county. For this is the very last place that Bill will think of looking for it."

"That's what *you* say."

"Besides," concluded Scoop, "this is the only thing we can do and play safe. For, as you say, we *would* get into trouble with the law if we actually stole the incubator."

Red gave the other a steady scowl.

"If this is borrowing," he growled, "peas is pickles."

"Red, you give me a pain. Yes, you do, for a fact. I actually believe you'd want to argue the matter if you were going to be hung."

"Huh!"

"You know as well as I do that the Cap'n would have raised Cain with us if we had told him the truth about the dodo egg. Let us borrow his incubator?—in a pig's eye! More than likely he would have run us out of the house on the end of his wooden leg. And, worse, he might have smashed the million-dollar egg into a thousand pieces."

The thought of my million-dollar egg being smashed into a thousand pieces gave me a sick, hollow feeling. As though the bottom had dropped out of my stomach.

"I'm glad we abducted it," I put in.

"Anyway," shivered Red, "let's hurry and get out of here. I'm scared to death we'll get caught."

I hung back to make sure there was enough oil in the incubator lamp to keep it burning for the next twenty-four hours. Then I followed the others up the ladder.

Suddenly the leader paused and hissed for us to back up.

"There's some one on the porch."

"The humpback!" breathed Peg, and I could feel a sudden quiver in his legs.

"Oh! . . ." gurgled Red, losing his grip on the ladder.

I caught him.

"Quick!" I cried. "Pull down the trap-door."

I don't mind telling you that I was scared stiff. For, with a million dollars at stake, I sort of had the feeling that the humpback would stop at nothing to recover the dodo egg.

And like the emperor gink who offered to swap his kingdom for a horse, I would have traded every penny of my million dollars just then for a husky iron bolt on the bottom side of the trap-door.

The humpback was now in the kitchen. We could hear him moving stealthy-like about the room. As though he had his shoes off. Plainly he was searching for the dodo egg. And it was not improbable that he would lift the trap-door.

"He's in the pantry," Scoop hissed in my ear.

"That's where the butcher knives are," I shivered.

There was a dead silence, both above and below.

"What's he doing?" whispered Scoop, as though his thoughts were snagged.

I jabbed him with my elbow.

"Keep still; he'll hear you."

Another year dragged by.

"Why doesn't he come out of the pantry?" persisted Scoop.

"Who wants him to come out?" I chattered. "*I* don't."

Peg was listening under a small window high up in the cellar's east wall.

"I can hear some one in the yard," he told us, in a low voice.

Thump! thump! thump! sounded a familiar peg-leg on the outside porch floor. A key turned in the door lock. The door creaked on its hinges.

"It's the Cap'n!" gasped Scoop, clutching my arm.

My shivers were drowned in a flood of bewilderment. For it was indeed Cap'n Tinkertop, whom I had carefully helped into bed earlier in the evening. At that time he had been unable to stand on his right leg. And now he was cheerfully humming to himself as he came briskly into the house.

I could conceive that in some miraculous way the leg pains had suddenly vanished. But why had he asked me to help him into bed, only to get up again when he was alone? And, in further mystery, where had he been?

A knife-edge of yellow light appeared in a floor crack directly over our heads.

"Um. . . ." mumbled the returned tenant. "Guess I'll have a cold biscuit a-fore I go to bed," and he pottered across the room.

All in an instant I realized his peril. And I tried to shriek a warning to him to keep out of the pantry. But I couldn't make my shrieker work. It was the sudden scare, I guess.

But Peg had his wits about him. He always does—good old Peg! He jumped for the ladder. The fact that he was running into danger didn't stop him for a single second. He has no fear. He's the bravest kid in Tutter, as I have said. And the best scrapper. He can play tunes on a comb, too.

There was a sudden scuffle of heavy feet on the rough pantry floor. Then we heard a gurgling scream, followed by the dull, sickening thud of a falling body.

Peg was now in the kitchen. And crowding down the fear that gripped me, I sprang up the ladder.

My chum was bending over a form on the floor. It was the Cap'n. He lay directly in front of the open pantry door. In a pool of blood. And there was blood on his face and head and shoulders.

Blood! The pool of blood that we had found in the haymow hadn't sickened me. But this did. I had the same gaggy feeling that I have when mother fries sauerkraut.

But I got all right when Peg told me that it was catchup and not blood.

Yes, sir, the Cap'n had been knocked out by a loaded catchup bottle. And the mysterious hump-back who had committed the deed had escaped into the night.

CHAPTER XI

THE HAIRY CATCHUP BOTTLE

I'M pretty smart on this first-aid stuff. For one time I studied up how to do it. That was when I was taking my scout tests. I know how to roll a drowned man on a barrel and how to rescue a smoked lady from a burning building and how to make a person come out of a sun fit and how to make a stretcher for a knocked-down and dragged-around flivver victim.

But the first-aid book that I had studied out of hadn't said anything about catchup bottles. And it was a puzzle to me now whether the Cap'n needed the catchup pumped out of him, as in a drowning case, or whether he needed fresh air pumped into him.

While I stood there undecided Peg got busy with a wooden spoon and sort of uncovered the roof of the victim's nose and bailed out his ears.

"Now," said he, "some one go over him with a wet towel."

As soon as the big one said "wet towel" I

found myself. I knew just what to do. And I ran to the bedroom bureau and selected a clean towel of the proper size. Then I carefully wet it in the kitchen water pail, exactly as the book said, and wrung it out.

I had to study a bit over the folding. For there's a difference between a head compress and a leg compress. One is made with four folds and the other with three. The trouble was I couldn't remember which was which.

Well, by the time I got the towel properly folded the Cap'n was sitting up.

"My haid," he groaned. "It hurts. An' they's vinegar in my eyes."

"It's catchup," explained Peg. "Don't blink. We'll dig out your eyes as soon as Jerry decides which end of the towel he's going to crochet first."

"Take it," I flared up, flinging the towel at the smart one.

There was a lively howl from the Cap'n at the time that his face was being mopped with the towel. And he jiggled his arms up and down like pump handles. Maybe he thought he was taking a swimming lesson. I don't know.

"How's that?" inquired Peg, squinting into the blinking brown eyes.

"They still smart," the old man complained.

"An' everything in my haid is goin' 'round an' 'round. Like a top. Somethin' hit me. I went to the pantry to git a—a——"

"Biscuit," I prompted.

"Uh-huh," he waggled. "It was to git a cold biscuit—one of your biscuits, Jerry. I—I went to the pantry to—to—— I went to the pantry—— Neow what *did* I go to the pantry fur?"

"To get a biscuit," I prompted again.

"Of course; of course. To git a biscuit. An' when I—I stepped into the pantry somethin' *jumped* at me." There was a short pause. "But it wasn't a biscuit," the dizzy one waggled slowly, trying to squeeze something out of his tumbled head. "No, it wasn't a biscuit. Fur it had hair on it."

"It was a catchup bottle," supplied Peg.

"Yes," the old man nodded in quick agreement, "it was a kaitchup bottle. An' it had hair on it."

Peg motioned to Scoop.

"He's out of his head. Take his other arm and we'll help him into bed."

Twenty minutes later we telephone to Doc Leland to come quick with his pill case. For the Cap'n was as crazy as a poisoned bedbug. Even as I stood at the telephone I could hear him shouting something about a catchup bottle with hair on it. In his crazy mind everything had hair on it: the bedstead and the bureau and the chairs and even the wallpaper flowers.

We tried to quiet him. But it was no use. So it was a relief to us when Doc rattled up to the front door in his loose-jointed flivver.

"Well," grunted the fat newcomer, waddling into the house, his straw hat in one hand and a shabby leather medicine case in the other, "what have you young hyenas bin up to this trip?"

Scoop shook his head.

"We didn't do it, Doc. Honest. A humpback did it."

Here the crazy one let out a screech. So Doc promptly peeled off his coat and hurried into the bedroom.

"Well, Cap'n," he rumbled, "how are you feelin' to-night?"

The wild look deepened in the brown eyes.

"It jumped at me, it did," the old man panted. "An' it had hair on it."

"He's talking about a catchup bottle," explained Scoop.

Doc wriggled his nose to settle his big spectacles and scowled.

"Nonsense! Whoever heard of a catchup bottle with hair on it."

"It jumped at me," babbled the wild-eyed invalid. "Jest like this," and he made a lunging, clutching motion with his long hairy arms.

"What jumped at you?"

"A kaitchup bottle. An' it had hair on it."

Doc flattened his lips and waggled.

"I've had 'em with yaller snakes an' pink elephants," he mumbled, puzzled by the case, "an' last winter when Miz Higgins had the lumbago she got the crazy idear in her head that she was a pullet an' tried to roost on the footboard of the bed. But this 'hairy catchup bottle' stuff is new in my practice. What does he mean, anyway?"

We couldn't answer the riddle. So, with a grunt, Doc set to work examining the bump on the injured one's head. He needed a basin of warm water, he said, and when Peg ran to the kitchen on the errand I took my chum's place at the bedside.

"Is his head cracked?" I inquired, feeling sick over the accident.

Doc grunted.

" 'Pears not to be. He got a' awful wallop, though."

"But he's crazy, isn't he?"

"Oh, he'll git over that all right."

"IT JUMPED AT ME, IT DID," THE OLD MAN PANTED.

Jerry Todd and the Purring Egg. *Page* 125

My mind had been troubled in the thought that indirectly I had helped to bring on the Cap'n's accident. You can see what I mean. We had brought the egg here in a trick; and the egg had brought the humpback. If we had left the egg in the cave the humpback never would have come here and hence the pantry accident never would have happened.

I wanted to go ahead and get my million dollars. But just the same I didn't want to have it on my conscience that in getting rich I had helped to put an old man crazy. So I was tickled pink, let me tell you, to learn from Doc that the Cap'n's crazy spell would go away in a day or two.

In my plans I already had given each of my chums fifty thousand dollars. That left me eight hundred and fifty thousand dollars. And now I decided in further generosity to give the Cap'n ten thousand dollars. That would square me with him. Yes, I went on in my generous streak, I might even give him a new flivver, or something like that, out of the eight hundred and forty thousand dollars that I had left. For certainly I wanted to do the right thing by him, considering his accident and my part in the earlier egg trick.

However, I sensibly checked myself up, I had

best go slow on my spending. For in a single day I had spent one hundred and sixty thousand dollars. At that rate my million dollars wouldn't last very long.

I watched at Doc's elbow while he washed the blue bump on the invalid's forehead and cut away the matted hair. Then he treated the injured spot with a strong-smelling liquid and got out his bandages.

"Now," said he in the completion of his work, grimly shooing us into the front room, "you kids kin limber up your under jaws an' tell me your story. But I warn you to stick to the truth an' tell me nothin' but the truth. Fur it'll go that much harder with you if you try to lie out of it."

"We wouldn't lie," Scoop spoke up for the four of us.

"No? Well, I'm glad to hear that. When did this accident happen?"

"About an hour ago."

"Was you kids in the house at the time?"

"We were *under* the house."

Doc couldn't understand that."

"No nonsense, young man," he scowled.

"We were in the cellar," Scoop explained, with a weak grin.

"What was you doin' down there?"

Here the leader went to the beginning of his story and told the other one everything that had happened.

"Um . . ." grunted Doc. "This is more serious than I thought. Calc'late I better git the police station on the 'phone right away. Fur this matter has got to be investigated proper."

Ten minutes later Bill Hadley, the town marshal, came heavily into the house. There isn't a gruffer or homelier man in the county than Bill. But he's well liked. And everybody says he's a good policeman. One time when we were Juvenile Jupiter Detectives we helped him solve the strange mystery of a vanished mummy. I told about that in my first book, JERRY TODD AND THE WHISPERING MUMMY. So he knows us. And usually he treats us pretty good.

But he looked anything but friendly to-night.

"I ought to put the hull kaboodle of you in jail," he roared, when he had heard our story. "Fur what you've done here to-night hain't nothin' short of burglary."

"We *had* to do it," defended Scoop. "It was our only chance to save the egg."

"That's a blamed poor alibi."

"We knew if we didn't hide the egg the humpback would get it away from us. And we didn't dast to take it out of the incubator, because that would have spoilt the hatching. Can't you see, Bill?—we just *had* to borrow the incubator."

"That kind of beggin' talk hain't a-goin' to git you no sympathy with me," growled Bill. "Fur I represent the law; an' what you've done here to-night is contrary to the law. So if the Cap'n lodges a complaint ag'in' you fur breakin' into his house you'll have to go to jail an' take your medicine."

"It'll be all right with the Cap'n," I spoke up quickly. "He lets us go in his house. Besides I'm going to fix it with him when I get my money."

"What money?"

"My million dollars."

Bill gave me a sharp look, as though to satisfy himself that I meant what I had said. Then he threw back his shaggy head and went, "Haw! haw! haw!"

"You won't laugh," I told him, "when you see me riding up and down Main Street in my new Packard roadster."

"Jerry, you're a scream. Does your pa know you're goin' to be a millionaire?"

"I'm going to surprise him."

The other straightened his face.

"Well, it's a fact I hain't got the nerve to put

you in the cooler, now that I know how influential you're goin' to be in a week or two," and he winked at Doc as though my riches were a big joke. "Fur a feller with a million dollars kin jest about run the town he lives in to suit hisself. An' I wouldn't want to offend you an' git put out of a steady policin' job. No, sir-ee!"

He was making fun of me. Some men like to do that with boys. Because they're bigger they think they're smarter. But I didn't say anything. I let him have a good time with me. I even pretended that I was as dumb as he thought I was. It was all right with me, I said to myself, if I could get on the good side of him.

"Yes, Jerry," he concluded in his smartness, "the thing fur you to do is to fix it with the Cap'n, as you say. That'll make it all right with me. Now bring a light, one of you. Fur I want to take a squint at this wonderful dodo egg. An' I want to see the hairy catchup bottle that the old man's ravin' about."

I held the lamp while the officer searched the kitchen for clews. Then I followed him into the pantry.

"What's this sticky pail doin' on the floor?" he grunted.

I told him it was the honey pail.

"The humpback must have knocked it down," I explained.

"Where was it?"

"Up there on the shelf," I pointed.

"Was there anything in it?"

I nodded.

Bill put the empty honey pail back on the shelf. And then he rounded us up in the parlor.

"I hope you kids are feelin' pretty gritty tonight. Fur I want you to show me the way to this cave where Peg seen the humpback. Calc'late that's where he hangs out. An' you kin help me arrest him."

"Hot dog!" cried Peg, his eyes snapping.

It was after twelve o'clock when we started for the cave. Bill had a gun and a pair of handcuffs. I had a lantern. The other fellows carried clubs.

It was moonlight. So we had no trouble finding our way. Turning into the ravine, we soon came to the dodo cave. But the humpback wasn't there. Nor could we find any trace of him in any of the ravine caves.

I don't know what made me think of looking in the nest where I had found the big egg. But I did. And what I saw there pretty nearly knocked me over, so great was my surprise.

Another dodo egg!

The others were waiting for me in the ravine. And in the moment of the second egg's discovery I yipped to them to come quick. It was Red, I think, who found the dodo tracks in the sand. We knew then that the encyclopedia was wrong in telling that the dodo birds were all dead.

Well, I sort of went dizzy in the face of my amazing good fortune. For it was easy enough to figure out how rich I was. If *one* dodo egg was worth *one* million dollars, certainly *two* dodo eggs were worth *two* million dollars.

Bill was on his knees beside the nest.

"It's lined with hair," he muttered, and held up a handful for examination. Then he turned to us with a queer look on his face.

I knew what was in his mind. He was thinking of the Cap'n's hairy catchup bottle.

Hair! Did dodo birds have hair, I wondered, or feathers?

CHAPTER XII

THE DODO HEN

Now, for several chapters in my story I haven't said very much about the Stricker gang. We had the tomato battle with them, as I have related. And later on we made the firecracker egg in the hope of scaring the wits out of them. But after that, with the clay egg put away to dry, the enemy had sort of dropped below our attention.

To explain this, a lot of very surprising things had happened. There was the hatching egg. That was an exciting thing in itself. At first, amazed and bewildered, we had come to believe that what we had thought in the beginning was a stone egg was in reality the newspaper's rejuvenated dodo egg. We didn't know *why* it had been brought to Tutter and left in the cave, unless, as I had suggested to Scoop, it had been put there by the rejuvenator in his secret work. Nor did we know the humpback's secret. The pool of blood on the haymow floor; the incubator fire; the stolen nest egg—these were not big things in themselves. But taken together in a chain they told a story of hidden purpose that baffled us.

Then in the past few hours we had busied ourselves in the hatching egg's abduction. After that had come the Cap'n's unfortunate accident. And also that same night, as I have written down, we had visited the dodo cave to arrest the humpback and while there I had discovered a second dodo egg, of the same size and apparently of the same weight as the first egg.

As I say, these were exciting adventures. And you can readily understand how the Strickers had come to be crowded out of our thoughts. But now they are to come back into my story again, though not in a big way.

Going back to where I left off, I was awakened the morning following our midnight trip to the dodo cave by a steady drip! drip! drip! on the porch roof just without my bedroom window. At first I sleepily thought it was Mother watering the lower porch boxes with the garden hose. Then in more complete wakefulness I realized that it was raining.

Ordinarily I like to lie and listen to the rain. It puts my mind full of pleasing pictures and fills me with secure contentment. But this morning I was cross about it. For it upset my plans to capture the dodo hen.

"Wake up," I growled, giving my snoring bedfellow a jab in the ribs.

"Huh?" gurgled Scoop, uncovering a pair of sleepy eyes. Then he braced himself on his elbows and squinted through the window into the dripping outside world. "Dog-gone!" he cried. "It's raining."

A thunder crash turned the cloud spigots wide open.

"The dodo hen won't be out to-day," I grumbled in disappointment.

My bedfellow laughed.

"Maybe our dodo hen will turn out to be a bob-tailed kangaroo."

"Kangaroos don't lay eggs."

"This may be a new kind of a kangaroo," he joked.

I thought of the hair-lined nest and the tracks that Red had discovered in the dodo cave.

"It's a dodo hen," I waggled, sure of myself.

"But, Jerry, the encyclopedia says the dodo hens are all dead. I told you so yesterday."

"They overlooked this one."

The other let his thoughts roam around for a few moments.

"Maybe you're right. Maybe there *is* a dodo hen around here. As a matter of fact it's easier for me to believe that than to believe this rejuvenation junk."

I grunted.

"You can change your mind quicker than a magician can change his shirt."

"What do you mean?"

"Yesterday you talked rejuvenation. And now you say it's junk."

"I'm better posted to-day."

I put my mind to work.

"But if the humpback isn't the egg rejuvenator that the newspaper told about, who is he?"

"It looks to me as though he's got an interest in the dodo hen—granting that there is one."

"Maybe he's the hen's husband," I joked.

"You're cuckoo!"

As I say, we had thought in the egg's hatching that it was indeed the newspaper's rejuvenated dodo egg. Now we knew differently. It was a fresh egg. And with the hatching thus explained, I felt foolish in the thought that I had taken stock in the "rejuvenation" story. That sure was the bunk.

There probably was not the slightest connection, we now agreed, between our egg and the rejuvenated egg—if there really was a rejuvenated egg, which was doubtful. The story that we had read in the newspaper was probably apple sauce, Scoop said. And it was just a coincidence that we had discovered two real dodo eggs at the time that the "rejuvenation" story was in circulation.

"Where did you say the dodo country is?" I inquired, in the course of our talk.

"Over near Africa. I forget the name of the island."

"Are there natives on the island?"

"Sure thing."

"What do you call 'em?—Dodoites?"

The other grinned.

"You can call them that if you want to."

"All right," I said quickly. "I've got the key to the puzzle. The humpback is a Dodoite. See? He's been keeping a dodo hen on the sly. Not even the encyclopedia people knew about it. And now he's brought the hen to this country."

"But why did he turn it loose in our hills?" puzzled Scoop.

"So that we could have the fun of capturing it," I laughed.

"Rats! If it's the last living dodo hen it's worth a pile of money. The man ought to know that, if he's got any sense at all. So why didn't he keep it instead of turning it loose?"

"Maybe it got away from him. And now he's searching the ravine for it. That's what he was doing yesterday when Peg saw him."

"But if his interest is in the dodo hen itself," further puzzled Scoop, "why did he come to the Cap'n's house last night?"

"He knew that the hatching egg was one of his dodo eggs and not a three-thousand-year-old rejuvenated egg, as we thought. And it made him sore, I guess, that we had the egg. He probably wanted to steal it or destroy it."

"But he didn't get the chance to do either—hey?"

"Bu-lieve me, he didn't."

The leader laughed.

"How about the second egg, Jerry? Are you going to hatch that one, too?"

"Why not?"

"Hot dog! This is fun. If we keep on, kid, we'll have a whole flock of dodo birds."

"With the hen and the two eggs," I counted, taking it for granted that the hatching would be successful, "we'll have three to start with."

"But we haven't got the hen yet."

"We'll get it to-day."

"Maybe—if it stops raining."

"It'll be fun capturing it."

"What if the old girl turns on us and kicks the pudding out of us?"

"You can't scare me."

"How big is a dodo hen, anyway?"

"You ought to know. For you're the guy who's been studying the encyclopedia."

The leader laughed again.

"We'd get a shock if something boiled out of the cave with six heads and as many legs."

"This isn't an octopus," I grunted.

"Who's going to put the salt on its tail?" he then inquired in nonsense.

"Red'll be a good one for that job."

"Then we better blindfold the poor dodo hen. For it'll die in fearful agony if it gets a look at his homely mug."

"Let's get up," I suggested, kicking the covers.

"Wait a minute. I want to think."

"About the dodo hen?"

"Sure thing. If we do capture it, Jerry, we ought to have a parade. We'll let you lead it into town. See? You're the best looking and the most dignified. You'll look swell up in front. And the rest of us will follow playing drums and horns."

"And then what?"

"We'll march all over town."

"Yah," I grunted, "and the first thing I know Bid Stricker'll get behind a bush and squash me in the mug with a rotten tomato."

"You can dodge."

"Let's cut out the parade," I advised.

"Shucks! If we can't have a parade, what good is the dodo hen, anyway?"

"We'll teach it tricks and get it a job in vaudeville."

"At a thousand dollars a week, hey?"

"You tell 'em!"

"Who gets the thousand dollars?"

"Me, of course."

"*You?* Say, whose dodo hen is this, anyway?"

"Mine."

"Like so much mud. If I help capture it I guess I own as much of it as anybody else."

"Who discovered the cave nest in the first place?" I reminded.

"Stingy!"

"You've got your nerve calling me stingy," I flared up. "How about that fifty thousand dollars?"

"What fifty thousand dollars?"

"The fifty thousand dollars I gave you yesterday."

"Go jump in the lake. You didn't give me fifty cents."

"But I promised you fifty thousand dollars. And that's just the same as giving you the actual money."

He turned up his nose at me.

"Wait till Peg and I get our dodo hen. You can have your old egg then. It won't be worth ten cents."

"*Your* dodo hen," I fired back. "How about the humpback? It's his dodo hen, if anybody happens to ask you. And he can make you give it up, too."

"How about your egg?" the other then fired back at me. "He owns that, too."

"Let's quit quarreling," I suggested to the leader.

He laughed.

"I wasn't quarreling. I was just kidding you. If we capture the dodo hen we do it together. All for one and one for all. That's us, kid."

"But the egg's mine," I reminded quickly.

"Sure thing. But don't have any wild dreams about it, Jerry. It was a million-dollar egg before the dodo hen showed up. But it isn't a million-dollar egg now."

I saw what he meant. And I was pretty blue

for a moment or two. A fellow can't help feeling blue to suddenly lose a million dollars.

Still, I hadn't definitely lost my fortune, I hung on. The dodo hen hadn't been captured yet. Maybe it never would be captured. And in that case my egg would complete its hatching and I would get my million dollars.

If only I could keep the dodo hen out of sight, I thought. If only I could keep my chums from capturing it.

In waking up I had grumbled over the rain, as I have said, for I had wanted to help capture the dodo hen and the rain had upset those plans. Now I was glad it was raining. I hoped it would keep on raining. That shows you how quickly things can flop around in a boy's life. One minute he wants to do something and the next minute he wants to do the opposite.

While we were dressing Scoop got his eyes on my second million-dollar egg.

"Don't let it skid," I cautioned, when he reached for it.

"It certainly looks like a stone," he mused, taking the big egg into the light for closer examination. "And *heavy!* Boy, it's the queerest egg *I* ever saw. No wonder we were fooled when we found the first one."

"Let me take it," I said, "and I'll hide it in the closet until we get ready to hatch it."

Here Mother called to us to come down to breakfast.

"The toast's getting cold, Jerry. So please hurry. And when you wash yourself don't forget the back of your neck."

"How about me?" Scoop called down the stairs. "Do I have to wash the back of *my* neck, too?"

"You most certainly do," laughed Mother, who is used to having my chums joke with her. "Otherwise you'll get no breakfast in *this* house."

CHAPTER XIII

SIX DODO EGGS

WITH breakfast awaiting us I became suddenly uneasy in the thought of facing Dad across the table. I knew he would ask me questions—he always does when I stay out late at night. And I was afraid this morning that his questions would lead up to things that I didn't want to talk about.

You see, I hadn't exactly obeyed him. And that is why I felt so guilty-like and so unwilling to face him. In talking with me he had pointed out my mistake in tricking the Cap'n. And, as you will remember, I had promised to go to my old friend with a frank confession of my wrong-doing and beg his forgiveness.

But when I had learned that the egg was hatching I had quickly decided to keep mum about our joke, though I knew at the time that I was breaking my promise to my parent and deceiving him. But I was sort of *greedy* to get my hands on the million dollars. And I was afraid that something would happen to the hatching egg if I went ahead with my promised confession.

Moreover, I had eagerly jumped into the abducting scheme with my chums to further assure the hatching egg's safety, though I had no intention of telling about that at home—at least not for the present. Of course, what I was doing was dead wrong. I fully realized that. It wasn't any credit to me to go back on Dad. For he was a good dad and always had been fair and square with me. But the temptation to get rich was too great for me to resist. Besides, I now let myself believe, dogged-like, that I had gone too far to turn back. I would keep on, I said, forgetting about Dad and what I owed him as a son. When I had the million dollars in my pocket he would forgive me. I would be able then to make him understand things. And instead of scolding me he would brag on me for my smartness in getting rich so young.

After these thoughts, it was a relief to me, as you can imagine, when no one appeared at the breakfast table besides us three. Dad was at the brickyard, Mother told me, where they were having more serious trouble with the big brick-cutting machine.

The rain continued to my fine satisfaction.

We would be drowned, I craftily told my chum, if we attempted to start for the dodo cave. It would be a foolish trip, I added. There were other days coming. However, Scoop insisted on going downtown. So we got raincoats and started out, picking up Red on the way.

When we came to the door of the police station the leader turned in. Bill Hadley wasn't at his desk. Nor was there a prisoner in any of the steel jail cages. So we knew the humpback hadn't been arrested overnight.

The marshal and another man came into the room while we were there. They were talking about Cap'n Tinkertop. And by keeping our ears open we learned, in some surprise, that our old friend had been removed from his home in Zulutown to the Tutter emergency rooms for better care.

"How did the accident happen, Bill?" quizzed Mr. Stair, the local newspaper man. "I collared Doc Leland down the street. But he grumpishly told me I'd have to get the story from you."

Bill dropped heavily into his desk chair.

"I can't tell you who did it, Stair, if that's the news you want. Fur it's a fact I don't know. I've got some clews, of course; an' I've got my own idears in the case. But I can't give you anything in that line fur publication. Not yet. You'll have to wait till I've made the arrest. Then you'll git the hull story."

But Mr. Stair wasn't easily sidetracked.

"Was it robbery?" he hung on.

"So fur as I know," Bill gave out guardedly, "the motive was robbery."

"Money?"

"No," and the speaker grinned at his thoughts, "it was honey."

"Honey?" repeated the puzzled newspaper man. "Did you say *honey?*"

Bill nodded.

"The only thing the man got away with was some honey; an' he took that away in his stomach."

Mr. Stair laughed.

"A thief with a sweet tooth, eh? Rather interesting. But isn't it possible," he followed up cleverly, "that the robber had his mind on the dodo egg? You know, Bill, a lot of people think that egg is the real stuff. And it wouldn't be at all surprising to have some crank get the notion of stealing it."

Bill shot us a signal to keep out of the conversation.

"Well, Stair, I can't tell you no more. Mebbe

the feller who beaned the Cap'n was after the dodo egg, an' mebbe he wasn't. We'll find out the truth when I git my man in bracelets."

When the newspaper man was gone the marshal gave us our orders.

"I want you kids to keep your traps shut," he scowled. "Don't you go tellin' nobody that you moved the incubator down cellar. Let the humpback think the egg is unprotected in the Cap'n's house. I'll be watching the house nights after this. An' if he comes back I'll git him. See?"

"We'll help you," cried Scoop, eager to take part in the exciting detective work.

"Um. . . . You kids kin best help me by keepin' your eyes peeled fur the culprit. If you git sight of him run in an' tell me. An' I'll do the rest."

I had a key to the Cap'n's house. So we went there in the rain to see how Humpty-Dumpty was getting along. The air in the cottage was heavy with a sour catchupy smell. I didn't like it. So I hurried down cellar. But somehow this morning the egg's distinct heartbeats didn't excite me into visions of great wealth, as had been the case the preceding day.

I was troubled over my fortune. And in feeling about in my mind for a scheme to save myself I wondered if I couldn't sneak away from my chums and go to the dodo cave with Dad's shotgun. If I could get a crack at the dodo hen everything would be lovely. For if the hen was dead the hatching egg would again be worth a million dollars.

Or, to another possible plan, if I could trap the dodo hen and secretly hide it in one of the unfrequented ravine caves that would fix me up all right. I rather preferred the second plan. For I don't like to kill things. Besides, Dad had given me orders never to use his shotgun. I was too young, he had said, to be trusted with a shotgun.

We didn't see anything of Peg that morning. And in the continued heavy showers I felt it would be useless for me to go to the dodo ravine. The dodo hen wouldn't be out.

Just before dinner I stopped at the emergency rooms to inquire about the Cap'n. His condition wasn't at all dangerous, the public health nurse told me, but he still was out of his head.

While I was standing in the hall the patient let out a screech. And again I took to wondering what he meant by a "hairy" catchup bottle. I thought of the dodo nest's hair lining, too. But whatever connection there was between the two I couldn't figure it out.

On rainy days we frequently play in the Meyers' barn. So we went there to-day. Red is a regular monkey at climbing around on the beams. Neither Scoop nor I could catch him in our tag game.

"Lookit!" cried the leader, when we were resting after a lively chase. "Here's our firecracker egg."

He took the clay egg down from its shelf, finding that it was hard and dry.

"Humpty-Dumpty, Jr.," he laughed.

"When are we going to play our trick on the Strickers?" I inquired eagerly.

The other's thoughts took a quick jump.

"Dog-gone!" he cried in disappointment. "We can't fool them now, for they don't even know that the incubator egg has disappeared. And we dassn't tell them it's gone."

"Why not?"

"Bill gave us our orders, didn't he? I guess yes! He said we were to keep still about the egg's disappearance. And if we start anything contrary to his orders we'll get in bad with him."

I laughed.

"Let's tell him about our firecracker egg. Maybe he'll help us in our trick. For he likes that kind of fun. You should hear him and Dad tell about the things they did when they were boys!"

But Scoop didn't like that suggestion.

"Oh, we don't need Bill's help. There are other days coming. And we won't be under obligations to him forever."

The sun came out in the middle of the afternoon. And straightway the leader wanted to hunt up Peg and head for the dodo cave. But I talked him down without arousing his suspicions.

My plan, of course, was to keep him and the others away from the cave until I had captured the dodo hen myself. For it would ruin me to have *them* capture it. You can see that.

I realized that there wasn't a moment to spare. So I got away from the others on a flimsy excuse and started for home. As I cut around the corner of the barn I saw Peg coming on the run. I could tell from his actions that something unusual had happened. So I hid in the alley close to the barn to hear what the newcomer had to say.

"What do you suppose those blamed Strickers did to me?" he shouted at Scoop and Red as he tumbled into the barn. "I had six dodo eggs and they got them away from me."

"Six dodo eggs?" cried Scoop. "Where in Sam Hill did you get six dodo eggs?"

"In the cave. I went there this morning in the rain."

"And you found six dodo eggs in the nest?"

"Sure thing."

"Six dodo eggs!" squeaked Scoop. *"Good* night! That old dodo hen will lay herself to death. *Wough!* Six eggs in one day. She's some layer, bu-lieve me."

"I was dragging the eggs home in a sack," Peg went on, "when who should I meet on the railroad track but Bid and his gang. We started sassing each other. And pretty soon they jumped on me and took me down. It was five to one. I didn't have a chance."

Scoop blew up.

"It's all Jerry's fault," he raved. "I wanted to go to the cave this morning—didn't I, Red?—but he said, no, it was raining too hard. And he stopped me this afternoon when it cleared up. Wait till I see him! I'll tell him a thing or two. For if he had kept his yap to himself I would have been with you. See? And then the Strickers wouldn't have dast to touch you."

Peg laughed.

"I feel sorry for Jerry.

"Huh! *I* don't."

"He thinks his dodo egg is worth a million dollars. But with six other dodo eggs in town the price is going to take an awful tumble, let me tell you. He'll find that his egg is worth about ninety-eight cents."

"What did the Strickers do with the eggs?"

"They've got 'em over at Bid's house, I guess."

"Can't we get 'em?"

"I don't know how. For we dassn't go in the house. But I can tell you this much—the first time I meet sweet little Biddy dear by his lonesome he's going to get *his*."

Scoop laughed.

"If we could only make him sit on our gunpowder egg while we touched off the fuse—hey?"

"Hot dog!" cried Peg. "I had forgotten about the firecracker egg. Let's see it."

The position of the sun told me that it was getting close to four o'clock. And with the big job ahead of me of capturing the dodo hen I skinned out for home to get ready. My chums' intended use of the firecracker egg didn't interest me now. It is fun to play jokes, of course; but when a fellow is fighting for his fortune, as I was, he can't be full of nonsense.

As Peg had said, my hatching egg wasn't worth a great deal now. There were seven other dodo eggs in town, counting the one I had at home. And there was no telling how many more the dodo hen would lay.

The thing to do, I told myself in grim determination, was to capture the hen without a moment's delay and put an end to its work. Later on I would get hold of the Strickers' eggs, if I could. I'd either hide them or destroy them. And I'd hide the second egg that I had found in the cave. My fortune then would be saved. For Humpty-Dumpty would be a million-dollar egg again.

Not knowing what the dodo hen was like, or how well it could fight in its defense, I decided I better wear thick gloves. And I got a catcher's mask to protect my face. In digging the mask out of my box of truck I found a football helmet. I put that on, too. Then I got a lasso rope and my slingshot and my air rifle and started out.

CHAPTER XIV

AT THE DODO CAVE

As I was leaving the house I met Mother coming home from shopping.

"For goodness' sake!" she puffed, staring at my dodo-capturing equipment as she took off her hat and tidied her hair. "What are you doing with all that truck? Are you looney?"

I laughed and fished around in her shopping bag.

"What have you got to eat?"

"Here's some cookies. *Stop it!* I didn't say you could take the whole bagful. Put some of those back."

"What's in here?" I munched, feeling of a package.

"That? Oh, it's some cloth I got in Stevenson's for a shirt for you." She gave the package closer inspection. "No, it isn't," she added quickly. "It isn't my package at all. I wonder if I didn't get Miss Mackey's package by mistake."

Miss Alleeta Mackey was the public health nurse.

"Let's open it," I suggested, curious.

But Mother shook her head.

"I'll telephone to the emergency rooms and ask the nurse if she has my package. She was in Stevenson's while I was there. We got to talking. And she told me among other things that Cap'n Tinkertop was sick and under her care. Did you know that, Jerry?"

I nodded.

"The poor old man," Mother went on, powdering her nose. "Miss Mackey said he was out of his head when they brought him to the emergency rooms this morning. Some one hit him over the head last night. But he's all right now."

"Hot dog!" I cried, tickled with the good news.

I was given a warm hug.

"You're a kind-hearted boy, Jerry; and a good boy, too. I'm proud of you."

I felt kind of mean and sneaking in her warm praise. I felt as though I wasn't deserving of it. And to avoid her eyes I grabbed my stuff and dug out.

As I was passing the emergency rooms I met old Caleb Obed hobbling down the steps with a checkerboard under his arm.

"Is the Cap'n well enough to play checkers?" I grinned.

"Um . . ." scowled the old man, motioning to me to get out of his way.

"What's the matter?" I laughed, guessing the cause of the other's ill humor. "Did he beat you this afternoon?"

"Um. . . . He's a ol' cheat, he be."

"I don't suppose *you* ever cheat," I reminded.

"He beat me to-day. But I beat him last night, I did." There was a cackling contented laugh. "He didn't git a game even at my house."

I stared.

"Was the Cap'n over at your house last night?" I inquired, surprised.

"From eight-thirty till ten-thirty."

"But how did he get over there? He had a lame leg."

"Lame leg? You mean a *peg*-leg."

"No, I mean a *lame* leg. Didn't he limp when he came into your house?"

"If he did I didn't notice it."

Here the old man hobbled past me. And left alone I stood puzzled in the street. Then the truth of the situation came to me. The Cap'n had lied to me about his lameness. That was it. His agony had all been put on. It was a scheme to get me to do his work for him while he took it easy.

I felt hard toward the tricky one at the moment. And I shut my eyes at the building where he was. I wouldn't go near him, I said, not even to get the true story of his attack in the pantry. I was through with *him*. Yes, sir-ee!

Clarks Creek touches the west end of Zulutown. And in crossing the bridge I noticed that the water was clay-colored from the day's heavy rains. One spring the creek was lifted out of its banks by a cloudburst, flooding Zulutown under three feet of dirty churning water. We had fun that day. For the separated wooden sidewalk made bully rafts. I fell in twice.

Bid Stricker lives close to the creek bridge. And at sight of his house I immediately thought of the six dodo eggs that were there. I wondered if I would ever be able to get my hands on them. It seemed doubtful.

"Jerry Todd," a woman called to me from the front door. "Will ye come over here a moment."

It was Mrs. Maloney, a neighbor of the Stricker family. You will remember her if you have read my second book, JERRY TODD AND THE ROSE-COLORED CAT. For she is the woman who gave us the milk for our hungry cats. We think she's all right. Certainly she was kind to us when we had our "cat farm" troubles. Everybody else laughed at us when the cats began to pour in from Chicago and Peoria and a dozen other cities. But she didn't laugh. And she was glad, too, when we solved the mystery of the rose-colored cat.

"Jerry," she called again, beckoning to me. "I want ye to come over here. I've got somethin' fur ye."

I was nervous about trespassing on Bid's property. As a rule I don't go in his yard. But he wasn't there now. So I took a chance.

"What do you want?" I grinned at the Irish woman.

"It's thim stone eggs of your'n, Jerry. Sure, it'll be doin' me a great kindness if ye'll stip in an' remove 'em from under me feet. I don't mind keepin' house fur a sick neighbor, an' with her pleurisy an' other pains Miz Stricker sure is in a bad way. But I see no need of stumblin' over a pile of stone eggs. Bah! The nonsense of luggin' home stone eggs!"

Well, I was dizzy in my sudden amazing good fortune. Scarcely more than ten seconds ago I had wondered if I ever would be able to get my hands on Bid's six eggs. It had seemed doubtful then. I hadn't the slightest idea how I was going to work it. And now the eggs were being shoved under my nose, as it were.

"Did you know that Bid hooked the eggs on Peg?" I inquired.

"Of course I know it. Fur didn't the tricky little divil come home braggin' about it? He's got 'em in the kitchen, Jerry. An' if he misses 'em when he comes home I'll tell him, 'An' who was it, young man, who hooked me ripe tomatoes the other night?' That'll settle *him*."

Mrs. Maloney is a good friend of mine, as I say. I do things for her. And I suppose, as my friend, it made her hot to think that Bid and his gang had piled on one of my chums. That probably was her reason in stopping me to give me the eggs.

Well, I made short work of dragging the eggs to the creek in a bag. And from the bridge I let them go kerplunk! into the middle of the stream. Boy, was I happy! I wanted to whistle and sing and dance all at the same time. Things were coming my way with a rush. I'd soon get my million dollars now.

The eggs destroyed, I legged it up the railroad track in the direction of the dodo ravine. The sun was gone now. Another storm was coming up. Running for the cave, I got there just in time. And did it *pour!* All I could think of was a giant wringing the clouds dry. It seemed impossible to me that there could be any water left up there.

The storm lasted for fifteen or twenty minutes. Then the sun came out again. I could see to move around in the cave now. And I went back to where the dodo nest was.

"For the love of mud!" I squeaked, staring at the hair-lined nest. "Eight more dodo eggs."

I blinked my eyes to make sure that I wasn't dreaming. But, no, I was wide awake. I was seeing things straight. There were eight new eggs in the nest at my feet. All of the same size and shape.

I sat down. For my knees were suddenly weak. Fourteen eggs in one day! Was this an ordinary day's work for the dodo hen, I wondered, dizzy. Or was it trying to kill itself on the nest?

As though there might be some magic connected with the eggs I touched them gingerly. They were real enough. And hard as stone. I lifted one. It was fully as heavy as the other two that I had found in the cave.

Having dropped Bid Stricker's eggs into the

creek as an easy and quick way of destroying them, I now decided to drop these newer eggs into the canal at the mouth of the ravine. But they were awkward things to carry. Two was all I could manage in a trip. Getting rid of the first load, I ran back to the cave for more—and what do you know if I didn't find *nine* eggs in the nest! While I had been away the dodo hen had staggered in with three more.

I was crazy now. I mean I was rattled. All I could think of was the need of drowning those eggs. So I grabbed two more and ran to the canal. I ran all the way back, too. I hadn't been gone more than four minutes. Yet I found *ten* eggs in the nest when I got back to the cave.

I gave up then. I saw it was no use. The thing to do, I decided, sweating, was to capture the dodo hen and put a padlock on its laying apparatus. Otherwise it might keep me toting new eggs to the canal for the rest of my life.

Getting my lasso, I hid outside in the rocks. I had my air rifle handy, and my slingshot. I had my gloves on, too, and my helmet and face guard. I was all ready for business.

My heart thumped as I lay there. I wondered what I would see. I had no idea what a dodo hen was like. But my imagination gave me a lot of exciting ideas. I was prepared to see anything in size from a goose to an ostrich.

An hour passed. I had seen nothing of the dodo hen. It probably had quit laying for the day, I decided. So I got busy on my job of toting eggs to the canal. I got rid of the ten eggs in five quick trips. The nest was empty now. And was I glad!

It came six o'clock. And still no sign of the dodo hen. But it was a cinch, I hung on, that the hen wasn't very far away, for it had been in the cave two times that afternoon that I knew of, though it had escaped me both trips. So the thing for me to do was to stay in the ravine within sight of the cave until the egg layer did show up. I'd miss my supper, of course. But that was nothing.

I was hopeful, though, that I wouldn't be kept in the ravine very late. Peg had seen the humpback there. I was afraid of the man. I didn't want to meet him in the dark.

CHAPTER XV

WHAT I DID

It got dark early. I wondered at this until a tongue of lightning came out of the black sky. Then I saw that still another storm was coming up.

It was deadly still in the ravine now. There wasn't a breath of air. Yet the leaves of the trees were quivering. With their heads high in the air, and their eyes turned on the rolling clouds, I could imagine that the big oaks and hickories were actually trembling in fear of their lives.

Once I walked a short distance north of the cave. And I heard a man's voice at the upper end of the ravine. It was Mr. Higbee calling to his cows. You will remember him as the man who owned this ravine. As I have written down in an earlier part of my story, Dad buys tons and tons of clay from the Higbee pit.

The rolling clouds were now directly overhead. So I got back into the cave to escape a drenching.

It was fearfully dark inside. I couldn't see the length of my arm. I didn't like it at all. It put my nerves on edge, sort of. But I had to endure it. It was that or go out in the storm.

And another such storm I never hope to see. The cave rocked under the thunder's blows. I wondered if I was safe. Certainly I didn't want the roof of the cave to fall down on me. *Good night!* That would be the end of me. And in alarm I got close to the entrance. Boy, the lightning flashes! Streams of fire. I had to keep my eyes shut.

The water was roaring down the bed of the ravine like a young river. And it was this, I think, that brought the town creek into my mind. Not since the last flood had we had such a downpour. And I knew well enough what was liable to happen to Zulutown within the next hour or two.

All in an instant I was made to realize the peril that Humpty-Dumpty was in. He lay in the path of the probable flood. The water from the raging creek would fill the cellar, snuffing out the incubator lamp. Thus chilled in his shell Humpty's heartbeats would come slower and slower. Finally the heart action would stop altogether. And that would be the end of him—

I WAS PREPARED TO SEE ANYTHING FROM A GOOSE TO AN OSTRICH.

Jerry Todd and the Purring Egg. *Page* 164

the end of my dream of owning a million dollars.

True, I had another egg. I hadn't completely forgotten about it. But somehow in the moment the second egg didn't count for much in my tumbling excited mind. I couldn't think of it as equaling Humpty-Dumpty in value. *He* was my million-dollar egg. *He* was my fortune. I had risked everything for him—I had destroyed twenty other dodo eggs in one day that he might be the world's only known dodo egg. I even had planned to get rid of the dodo hen if I could capture it. All this I had done to save my first egg. And now I stood a big chance to lose it. It all depended on whether I got to it first—or the flood.

With no thought of the storm, and completely forgetful of the dodo hen now, I tumbled out of the cave and ran down the ravine to the railroad track. The lightning was a big help to me. It kept me from knocking trees down. Also it kept the humpback from knocking *me* down.

I don't know how long I was on the railroad track. Maybe twenty or thirty minutes. I couldn't run very fast. The ties tripped me up. After a couple of hard falls in the dark, in which I bent the rails out of shape with my head, I slowed up.

I was gasping when I came to the creek bridge into Zulutown. And I clung to the railing to get my wind. Then I tumbled on.

Across the bridge the flood got me around the legs. Shouting voices came out of the darkness. I could see jumping lanterns and, in the light of these lanterns, splashing forms of men and women in rubber boots and rubber coats. It was the Zulutown people getting out of their homes to higher ground.

I had a time getting the Cap'n's door unlocked in the dark. In my crazy excitement I tried to use the key every which way except the right way. You know how it is with a fellow in a moment like that. The harder he tries to do a thing right the more he fumbles.

Lighting a kitchen lamp to see what I was doing, I threw up the trap-door. A fearful roar came out of the black cellar. It was the water pouring in through a window.

I didn't stop to find a foothold on the ladder. I just clung to the sides and slid. That was the quickest way to get down. Slivers stabbed my fingers. But that was nothing.

Landing waist deep in the water, I stopped dead still and sharpened my ears. For I had detected a queer splashing sound. It wasn't the flood. It sounded more like something thrashing around in the rising water.

Sewer rats!

Well, as Red said afterwards, it might have been worse—snakes, for instance, or hungry alligators. But on the other hand I want to tell you it could have been a lot better. I guess yes! For the only thing I hate worse than a rat is two rats.

But scared as I was of getting a hunk bit out of me I didn't back up. For I realized that if I deserted Humpty-Dumpty I would lose everything I had been fighting for. The thing for me to do if I wanted to save my fortune was to forget about the rats and hustle Humpty out of the cellar into dry quarters. I had to do that or lose my million dollars.

So I forced the wabble out of my legs and made a gritty lunge for the incubator. In another moment I had a grip on Humpty-Dumpty. I held him out of the water, which was now up to my armpits.

It was no easy job getting back to the ladder. The whirling water sort of lifted me from my feet and tipped me up. Also I had to dodge the swimming rats.

But I made it. I got to the ladder and dragged myself out of the water into the kitchen. I sort of staggered. My clothes were sopping wet. They hung on me like lead.

Humpty-Dumpty was cold and sticky. I tried warming him over the lamp. But that didn't work. Then I thought of the Cap'n's hot water bottle. Just the thing! I got busy with cobs and kerosene and built a fire in the kitchen stove. And when the water was steaming in the kettle I ran to the front bedroom to get the rubber bottle. But it wasn't in its regular place in the top dresser drawer. Nor could I find it in any of the lower drawers, or anywhere in the bedroom. I was up against it.

Still, there was the stove. It was giving out heat, and heat was what I needed. I could make a sort of incubator of the oven, I decided. Dashing into the kitchen, I felt of the oven's heat. It was just about right, I figured, for a hatching egg. So I quickly wrapped a dish towel around Humpty and chucked him into his new nest, hoping that he would be all right again when the heat got into his shell.

My clothes needed wringing out. So I started to undress beside the fire. But suddenly I went stock-still in the feeling that I was being watched. Like the night in the barn. Standing there in my shirt-tail, I could imagine that a pair of outside eyes were boring holes in me.

I realized my danger. The humpback had come back for his egg. I didn't want to fall into his hands. I guess not! He had tried to kill the Cap'n and now he might try to kill me. My life was worth more to me than a million dollars. He could have his old egg for all of me. I had fought for it until I hadn't any fight left. Yet in the thought that it was lost to me forever I was sick with despair.

To get out of the humpback's way I grabbed the hand lamp and flipped myself into the pantry. I slammed the door shut and put my weight against it. There was a dead silence for two or three minutes. Then I heard stealthy footfalls. It was the man tiptoeing into the house. Now he was in the kitchen. The floor boards creaked under his weight. Gee-miny crickets, he must be a big guy! I thought of how small *I* was.

Splash! I gave a startled cry. Then quick as scat I realized what had happened. The trapdoor had been left open and in the darkness the humpback had fallen into the water-filled cellar.

Darting from the pantry, I slammed the trapdoor shut. I did it in a flash. Then, panting and shaking and half scared out of my wits, I fell flat on my stomach. For the trap-door had no latch on the upper side. And the only way I could keep it closed on my prisoner was by holding it down with my weight.

CHAPTER XVI

THE END OF POOR HUMPTY-DUMPTY

PROBABLY right now you're saying to yourself that what I did was a very brave act. You're thinking of the big risks I ran in capturing the humpback. And you're probably wondering where I got the courage to do it.

As a matter of fact I really didn't realize what I was doing at the time. I was sort of crazy. I just jumped into the thing. If I had stopped to figure out what was liable to happen to me as a result of the act I probably wouldn't have done it. I wouldn't have had the nerve. And that's a fact.

For I was tackling a man. A great big fellow. I knew he was big by the way the kitchen floor had creaked under his weight. And you must remember that I was only a boy; and a pretty small boy, at that. With my light weight I wouldn't last very long if the trapped one took a notion into his head to force up the trap-door, as could be expected of him.

But, as I say, I just rushed into the act without realizing what I was doing. And with the trap sprung on my prisoner, as it were, there I lay on the trap-door, panting and quivering and wondering, dizzy-like, what was next on the exciting program.

Instead of holding down the trap-door I should have run home with the million-dollar egg. I could have gotten away with it in the time that the humpback was crawling out of the cellar. But that thought never came to me. We had talked about the humpback's capture. I had it on my mind. And now all I could think of was the necessity of holding him for the law.

Sprawled on the trap-door, I could hear the prisoner splashing around in the water. But he gave no outcry. That was queer, I thought, straightening out my senses. Why didn't he let out a yip? Certainly if it had been me in the cellar—with those rats!—I would have yipped my head off. I guess yes! And why, I wondered further, didn't he put his shoulders to the trap-door and do some work? Couldn't he find the ladder in the darkness?

Then came the awful thought that the captive's lungs were filling with water and he couldn't yell. I didn't want him to die in the cellar. For if he drowned, or was bit to death by rats, I would be a murderer. Yes, I would. For I had trapped him in the cellar. I had shut him in. Still, I didn't dast to let him out of the cellar to save his life. For if I did that he might murder *me*.

My tumbling thoughts were suddenly lifted to Humpty-Dumpty when I noticed the stove's open draft and red-hot lids. Gee-miny crickets! My million-dollar egg—or, to put it another way, the egg that was mine again in the humpback's capture—would be baked to a crisp if I didn't snatch it out of the oven. I started for the stove. But I got back to the trap-door in a jiffy when I heard the hinges creak.

You can see what a fix I was in. If I left the trap-door, even for a moment, the humpback would climb out of the cellar and go for me. And if I didn't get Humpty-Dumpty out of the blistering oven I would lose my million dollars this time for good.

I had a bigger job than I could handle. I needed help. I realized that. So I promptly let out a yip. And maybe you think I wasn't glad when I got an answering cry. Oh, boy!

"Come quick!" I screeched, as the trap-door began to jiggle.

I could hear the flood workers splashing toward

the house. They had lanterns, as I could tell by the light through the window. Now they were in the yard. But I didn't suspect who was coming to my rescue until Dad and Bill Hadley stamped into the house in their dripping hip boots.

"Here comes the rescue party," Dad sang out. "All aboard for dry land. Get your Sunday clothes and all your valuables." Then he got his eyes on me in my shirt-tail and blinked in surprise. "What the dickens? . . ." he cried. He sort of caught his breath and took hold of me. "What's the matter, Jerry? What are you doing here?"

"I've got him captured," I screeched, hanging to the trap-door. "I've got him shut in the cellar."

"You've got who shut in the cellar?"

"The humpback."

Bill laughed.

"Are you sure, Jerry, it hain't the dodo hen?"

For answer I pulled up the trap-door. I had no fear of the captured humpback now. For wasn't Dad there to help me? And what do you know if I didn't find myself staring, dumfounded-like, into the dripping face of a big brown bear! Yes, sir, what I had captured wasn't a man at all. It was a bear. I guess I would have tumbled backwards in a heap if Dad hadn't steadied me.

Well, there isn't much more to tell. As Scoop said the following day, when he treated me to ice cream in Wheeler's drug store, our adventure really ended with the capture of the escaped performing bear. Its name was Beppo, or something like that. And it belonged to the humpback, a gypsy. He came into town shortly after the animal's capture and took it away with him. But first he made it do its tricks for us. It was a pretty smart bear, I want to tell you.

It was the escaped bear that had been hiding in the barn and not the humpback, as we had supposed. The pool of blood had come from a cut in one of the animal's feet. Why it tipped the incubator over, thereby setting fire to the barn, we'll never know, for bears can't talk to explain their actions. Nor will we ever know why it stole and hid the china nest egg. Maybe it liked eggs and thought the nest egg was a hen egg. That's the only explanation I can offer.

And our dodo egg? Well, it wasn't a real egg, after all. It was a hunk of baked clay. I found that out when I dropped it on the floor, after having rescued it from the hot oven. It broke into a dozen pieces. And when I saw what was inside of it . . .

Well, I haven't been very thick with old Cap'n

Tinkertop since he played that trick on us. Still, I guess we deserved what we got handed to us. For we started it. But it wasn't any fun to have the whole town laughing at us. I guess not! And to this day people stop me in the street and quiz me about my million dollars. They think it's smart.

I'll admit I was something of a dumb-bell to think that I could get a million dollars out of a dodo egg. I realize now what a crazy thought it was. My imagination played a trick on me, I guess.

Still, I should worry about that. As I told Dad that night when we got home from Zulutown it was more fun to be just myself and know that I was on the square with him and my chums than it was to be a young millionaire with a troubled conscience. Anyway, riches are a bad thing for a boy. I found that out.

In our talk I told Dad how sorry I was for what I had done. And I further told him how it had troubled me to think that I had gone back on him for money. He said he understood. And big as I am—and I have a long-pants suit, I want you to know—he took me on his lap and held me tight and rubbed my head with his nose. That's a chummy trick of his. He said I was all right. As for the million dollars, we didn't need the money, he said, for we already had one millionaire in the family. He meant himself. "I've got you, Jerry," is the way he bragged on me, "and you're worth a million dollars to me any day in the week."

I tell you I've got a swell dad. I guess I won't ever go back on him again for *anything*. No, sir-*ee!*

Oh, yes! The afternoon I sneaked away from my chums and went to the dodo cave they "planted" the firecracker egg on Bid Stricker. He was sore over the loss of his six eggs—the ones I had drowned in the creek. So he was tickled to find the new egg. He lugged it home and put it in an old incubator. *He* was going to have a hatching egg, too, he bragged. Well, the incubator caught on fire and the egg blew up. *Bang!* Bid was scared out of his wits. He ran around the block so fast that he met himself coming back.

If you think the explosion wasn't funny, you should hear Peg tell about it.

Maybe I should write down in conclusion that it was Bobby and Betty Higbee who put the clay eggs in the cave nest, which they had lined with hair from one of their cow's tails. I don't know *why* they did it, unless they had been reading about Mr. Andrews' five-thousand-dollar dinosaur eggs. They're great kids to make up games. In this game they even made fake animal tracks near the nest. They worked it slick, all right. It's a cinch *we* were fooled.

So you see there was no connection between the "hairy" catchup bottle and the hair-lined nest. The Cap'n had seen the bear in his pantry and that is what he meant in his rambling talk about a "hairy" catchup bottle. He really didn't know what he was saying.

We wondered how the old man had tumbled to our joke. And when we got the truth from him Scoop felt pretty cheap. The final paragraph of the Humpty-Dumpty letter, which invited the inventor to send his photo to Chicago, was the weak part of our scheme. That was some of Scoop's smartness. He never dreamed, of course, that the Cap'n would actually send one of his pictures away.

But that is exactly what the old gilly did. Imagine! And when the package came back stamped "no such address" he immediately suspected that he had been tricked by us. Learning the truth about the incubator egg, he then had made an egg of his own—a purring egg with a small alarm clock inside of it—and the story of his lame leg was just a stall to get us to do his housework for him while he took it easy, laughing at us up his sleeve. *That* was *his* idea of paying us back.

There's no telling how long he would have let us slave for him if he hadn't met with his accident, to be then taken away from home. He intended keeping up the trick as long as he could, using a new boy each day so that he would get a crack at all of us. But I guess he couldn't have fooled us many days in succession. For we're pretty smart.

That is all *I* have to tell you. But don't stop here. Eddie Blimke is going to tell you now about his "Humpty-Dumpty" lodge. His story starts on the next page. You'll want to read it. For there's a lot of fun and surprises in it. What he says, and what I have written down, really go together.

And look for me soon in still another book, JERRY TODD IN THE WHISPERING CAVE.

THE SECRET ORDER OF HUMPTY-DUMPTY, THE REJUVENATED EGG

By

EDDIE BLIMKE

I CAN'T write as good as Jerry Todd. He's had a lot more practice than me. But I've been asked by the publishers of this book to tell in my own way about our Lake Ripley "fun" lodge, *The Secret Order of Humpty-Dumpty, The Rejuvenated Egg,* so I'll sharpen my pencil and do the best job I can.

I asked the publishers why they didn't have Jerry Todd tell about our "fun" lodge. But, no, they wanted *me* to tell about it, they said, for I had helped to get it up.

And I guess they're right, all right, when they say that this book of Jerry Todd's wouldn't be complete without some one like me telling how we used the "egg" idea in our lodge. As a matter of fact we wouldn't have had a secret

"Humpty-Dumpty" lodge if it hadn't been for the egg story. What Jerry Todd has told in the preceding pages and what I am going to tell go together. There's no doubt about that. And if you have had fun in reading the story you'll probably enjoy hearing about our lodge, too.

You see, to start with, I heard this story of the "purring" egg before it was put into a book. That is, I was one of a gang of kids to whom the author read the story aloud. My dad has a summer home at Lake Ripley, near Cambridge, Wisconsin, and that is where Edward Edson Lee spends his summers. Mr. Lee is an author. He writes books for boys. This is one of his books, only it has the name of Leo Edwards on the cover. Some authors, you know, have a pen name, as they call it, and Leo Edwards is Mr. Lee's pen name.

Well, as you can imagine, we hang around Mr. Lee's cottage quite a lot when we're at the lake. He's jolly and always ready for fun. He likes kids. Whenever he finishes a new book he sends word to us, up and down the lake shore, and that night we crowd around him on his front porch while he reads the book to us. Only it isn't a book then, it's what he calls a manuscript. So now it's clear to you, I guess, how I came to hear the "purring egg" story before the book people got hold of it to publish it.

And was I lucky? *I* think so. I guess it isn't every kid who has a chance to hear a real author read his books aloud before those books are published. We like Mr. Lee for what he does for us. Outside of my dad I like him better than any man I know of. And you would like him that way, too, if you knew him as well as I do.

His summer home is called Hi-Lee Cottage. It's on a hill, and that is where the "Hi" part comes in. Our cottage—the Blimke cottage, I mean—is called Elmhurst, because in the winter time I live in Elmhurst, Illinois. I have a brother and two sisters. I'm the oldest. Mary comes next, then Billy, then Dorothy.

Well, one day Mr. Lee stopped me on the lake when I was exercising my canoe and told me that a new boy was coming to visit him.

"His name is Herb Isham, and he's the only son of an old chum of mine of the same name," Mr. Lee said. "It's Herb, senior, and Herb, junior."

"Just like me," I said. "I'm the 'junior' in our family."

There was some more talk about Herb.

"How old is he?" I asked.

"Sixteen. And he lives in Oglesby, Illinois," said Mr. Lee.

I grinned at that. For that was some name for a town, I thought.

"When Herb comes," I said, "I'll drop in and give him the 'once over.'"

"I want you to do that," said Mr. Lee. "While he's here I'd like to have you make a pal of him. He's a good kid. And he's about your age, and everything."

"Hasn't he ever been here before?" I inquired, checking over in my mind the different boys I had met at Hi-Lee Cottage. I couldn't remember a boy named Herb, though.

"No," said Mr. Lee. "This is his first trip to Lake Ripley. I've had some letters from him; and he calls me Uncle Ed, as I want him to. But I've never seen him and he hasn't seen me."

The following Monday morning Herb arrived in style in his pa's shop-worn Lizzie, and I had the honor—ahem!—of shaking his mitt. I wanted to ask him if he was the mayor of Oklesby, or whatever the name of his town was. But I kept shut. I didn't want him to think that I was fresh—not right at the start.

I saw he was a pretty good kid. Kind of good-looking, too. I figured I wouldn't be ashamed to introduce him to my sister, Mary, or to the girls I knew in Cambridge.

Having introduced me to his famous "nephew" from Oglesberry, Mr. Lee gave me the wink.

"Now, Eddie," said he, "you can take Herb out fishing, if you will, and show him which end of the pole to put his line on and how to bait his hook without getting it caught in the seat of his pants. He's pretty smart at picking up things. You'll find that out. And very likely you won't have to show him your stuff more than once. But whatever you do don't let him try to row the boat. He never saw a rowboat before and he might fall into the lake and spoil the fishing."

That made Herb grin. For he knew, of course, that he was being joshed. He wasn't green about fishing. He had done a lot of fishing at home. I learned that later on. And he knew how to row a boat, too. In fact, as I found out, he was an all-around kid. That is why I took a shine to him. And that is why I like him so well to-day.

He took me in his room and showed me his fishing tackle. He had just bought a lot of new bobbers and casting plugs done up in fancy colors and he felt pretty proud of his truck. So I bragged on it, of course. Then we went fishing.

I don't remember whether we got any fish that day or not. It doesn't matter. What I am going to tell you about, instead of fish, is how we initiated Herb. Hot dog! We had fun that night. I'll never forget it.

Here's the way it came about: Herb had a two-week's vacation. And along toward the tail-end of his visit I got to thinking that we ought to do something to him to have some fun with him. For he had pulled off a lot of funny stuff on us. He thought he was pretty cute.

"I know what we'll do, Eddie," Mr. Lee told me, when I talked with him to get some ideas. "We'll get up a lodge and initiate him."

"What kind of a lodge?" I said. "The Junior Order of Lake Ripley Rascals?"

"Remember my book about the rejuvenated egg?" said Mr. Lee.

"Sure thing," I said.

"All right," said Mr. Lee. "We'll call our lodge *The Secret Order of Humpty-Dumpty, The Rejuvenated Egg.*"

"And do we pretend that Herb is a rotten egg," I said, "and crack him over the head with a 'hairy' catchup bottle?"

"Oh, no," said Mr. Lee. "We won't want to

knock him cuckoo, like poor Cap'n Tinkertop. Let's save him for another year."

"What do we do?—throw him in the lake with his clothes on?"

"I wonder," said Mr. Lee, "if we can't surprise him."

"If you'll tip him over," I said, "and give me leave to use a paddle on him I bet *I* can surprise him."

"Let's not get rough in our initiation," said Mr. Lee. "For the neighbors will come in to see the fun. And we will want to remember that we are gentlemen and not rough-necks."

"What's your idea?" I said.

"I'll think about it and make some notes. And then we'll get together and work the thing out."

Well, the next morning Mr. Lee told me that he was all ready for my help. I was to get another boy, he said, and the three of us were to be the organizers and charter officers of the new lodge.

I hunted up Dick Hippenmeyer. He lives next door to me on the lake shore in Sleepy Hollow Cottage. When I told him about the new lodge, and how we were going to help Mr. Lee get it up, he was tickled pink.

That morning in Mr. Lee's studio we got everything down on paper. We had a lot of stunts framed up. In the afternoon we had a rehearsal. And that night—oh, boy, how well I remember it!—we had the big initiation.

But first, before putting on the initiation, we sent notes to the three boys who were going to be initiated. The victims were Jerry Todd, John Gray (an Elmhurst kid) and Herb. Here is the note Herb got:

> Herb Isham: It has been reported to our most notable juvenile lodge, *The Secret Order of Humpty-Dumpty, The Rejuvenated Egg,* that you are something of a bad egg. As it is our job in this summer community to make bad eggs good, through our secret processes of rejuvenation, you are cordially invited to appear this evening at Hi-Lee Cottage at eight-thirty to undergo examination. If we find in our examination of you that there is hopes for you, we will proceed with the initiation and take some of the "badness" out of you.
>
> (Signed)
>
> Most Excellent Humpty-Dumpty
> Keeper of the Keys
> Captain of the Court

Jerry Todd rode the goat first. While we were initiating him John Gray and Herb were put on their honor to row into the lake and stay there, out of hearing of what was going on in the cottage, until we called to him. When Jerry had been "rejuvenated" we took John and "rejuvenated" him. Herb came last. I'll tell you just what we did to him. I'm going to tell you what our lodge work is, and everything. The publishers of this book want me to tell everything. So if you, as a reader of the book, want to get up an initiation of your own, you'll have our stuff to go by. See? You can use any of our stuff that looks good to you; or you can take part of it and make up some new stuff. It's easy. But, as Mr. Lee said when we were getting up our lodge, it is better to use stunts that *surprise* the candidate, rather than rough stuff. You'll better understand what I mean as you read into the initiation.

Well, the house was full of people. My mother and dad were there, and my brother and sisters and all the neighbors. The chairs in the big living-room were arranged along the walls, as in a regular lodge room. As Humpty-Dumpty, Mr. Lee had his station at one end of the room and my station—I was Keeper of the Keys—was at the other end of the room, close to the kitchen door. I mention the kitchen for that was the

Outer Chamber of our Castle—the place where we got the candidates ready for initiation.

But before we dressed Herb up for the initiation, Mr. Lee said to him in the Outer Chamber:

> Herb Isham, you are among friends to-night. You are *my* friend—my very dear friend, I will say—and it is my pleasure to inform you that in our initiation of you into our lodge we will do nothing of an ungentlemanly nature—we do not propose to get rough with you or to harm you in the slightest way. In fact, in our lodge room are many adult friends of yours, women and men of this community, and this should convince you that we have no thought of being rough with you. Are you willing therefore to let us complete our friendly initiation of you without acting stubborn or offended; without attempting to unhoodwink yourself; and without struggling with your conductor or acting rough or ungentlemanly? Unless you answer "yes" we cannot proceed with the initiation. Do you answer "yes"?

Herb said "yes." And he was kind of quiet about it, too. He had held to the idea that we were going to "rough-house" him. And he had it all figured out, I guess, how he was going to fight back. But now, in our promise to use him right, we had him guessing.

Well, we blindfolded him. Then we put a kimono on him—a real fancy one, let me tell you—and we tied fancy ribbons on his arms and ankles. He sure looked like a lulu when we got through with him.

He was scared now. While he was the village cut-up around the kids he was by nature kind of bashful around grown-up people, and it got his goat now to think that he was going to make a show of himself in girls' clothes. But he didn't back down.

Well, with the weak-kneed candidate all lit up for the parade, Humpty-Dumpty opened the lodge in formal style.

"Keeper of the Keys," said he.

I got up at my station and saluted with the official Boy Scout salute.

"Yes, Most Excellent Humpty-Dumpty," I said.

"I am about to open our lodge," said Humpty-Dumpty. "And in our regular custom you will so inform the charter members and guests."

You see, to explain, the "charter members" were the people who had been invited to see the initiation. As I say, the house was full of people. We let the girls in. But not the big boys. We'd initiate them later on, we planned.

Well, I went on with my part in opening the lodge.

"Charter members and guests," I said, "I have been instructed by our Most Excellent Humpty-Dumpty, the senior officer of this lodge, to inform you that our lodge will now be opened. And in our regular custom, at three taps of my gavel, you will arise and face the Most Excellent Humpty-Dumpty to receive his charges."

Here I gave three taps with my gavel. And all the people in the lodge room got up except Humpty-Dumpty.

"Charter members and guests," said Humpty-Dumpty, "before we can proceed with our planned initiation it is necessary for me, as the senior officer of this lodge, to pledge you to keep the secrets of our most notable juvenile order, as these secrets will be revealed to you to-night. If you are willing to give this promise of constant secrecy, you will raise your right hands."

Everybody in the room responded.

"Keeper of the Keys," Humpty-Dumpty then said to me, "the promise has been given. Accordingly you will seat the charter members and guests by one tap of your gavel."

I gave the ordered tap, seating the people, and then I sat down, too.

In the Outer Chamber, which was the kitchen, the Captain of the Court, who was Dick Hippenmeyer, had heard us open the lodge. And now, with the lodge opened, he got busy on his part in the work.

"Herb Isham," said he to the candidate, who now held a croquet mallet on his left shoulder and a heavy iron maul on the other shoulder, "you are about to enter the Castle of our Most Excellent Humpty-Dumpty. I will give the secret signal on the Outer Gate that will gain admittance for us. Should you at any future time want to gain admittance to our Castle you will use the same signal, which is given with one long rap, four quick raps, and two long raps. Please listen while I give the signal and remember it."

The raps were given and I got up and saluted.

"Most Excellent Humpty-Dumpty," I said.

"Yes, Keeper of the Keys," said Humpty-Dumpty.

"I have reason to believe that our esteemed Captain of the Court has returned from his long journey, for I hear a signal at the Outer Gate of our Castle."

"That is well," said Humpty-Dumpty. "It has been many days since our esteemed Captain of the Court went abroad in quest of the Lost

Egg. You will answer the summons at our Outer Gate, to learn if it is indeed our returned Captain of the Court. If so, you will report his tidings to me."

Getting these orders, I rattled a chain to make it sound as though the door was fastened with heavy chains. Then I opened the door, facing the Captain of the Court and the candidate. And when I saw Herb standing there in his fancy kimono, with the croquet mallet on one shoulder and the big maul on the other, I thought I'd die. He sure looked funny. We had had some high old fun initiating Jerry Todd and John Gray. But I knew we were going to have more fun with Herb. For he was the kind of a kid you could have fun with.

"Who comes here?" I said in a deep impressive voice.

"Your most humble brother, Captain of the Court," said the candidate's conductor.

I leaned forward, putting my hand over my eyes. You see, I was supposed to make sure that it really was the Captain of the Court who was trying to get into the Castle, and not some impostor, or whatever you call it. You know what I mean.

"It is indeed my esteemed brother, Captain of

the Court," I said. "What are your tidings, good brother?"

"It is my pleasure to report success," said the Captain.

"Then you have found the Lost Egg!" I said, acting excited and pleased.

The Captain showed off the cunning little candidate.

"Here it is," said he.

I looked the kimono rack over and turned up my nose.

"What!" I said in disgust. "Is this the Lost Egg? It looks more like a nut to me than an egg."

"I assure you, most esteemed brother," said the Captain, "that it is indeed the Lost Egg."

I got ready to close the door.

"You will await here," I said, "while I inform our Most Excellent Humpty-Dumpty of your tidings."

Then I closed the door and rattled the chain.

"Most Excellent Humpty-Dumpty," I said, saluting.

"Yes, Keeper of the Keys," said Humpty-Dumpty.

"It is my pleasure," I said, "to report to you

that our esteemed Captain of the Court is indeed without the Outer Gate of our Castle."

"What are his tidings?" said Humpty-Dumpty.

"He brings good tidings," I said. "He has found the Lost Egg."

"Good!" said Humpty-Dumpty. "You will admit our esteemed Captain of the Court and submit the Lost Egg to examination."

Getting these orders, I rattled the chain and opened the door.

"It is my orders from our Most Excellent Humpty-Dumpty," I said, "to admit you to our Castle."

Here the Captain led the candidate into the lodge room by the arm. I shut the door and sat down. At the other end of the room Humpty-Dumpty switched on a talking machine, playing *The Parade of the Wooden Soldiers*, and the candidate was led two times around the room in time to the music, stopping at my station. Then, of course, the music was stopped.

"Cock-a-doodle-doo," said the Captain.

"Cut-cut-ca-daw-cut," I said.

"Here, my brother," said the Captain, "is the Lost Egg."

"What seeks he here?" I said.

"Initiation into our most notable juvenile order," said the Captain.

"What is his name?" I said.

"Herb Isham," said the Captain.

"Where did you find him?" I said.

"In an ash can in Oglesby," said the Captain.

"How old is the candidate?" I said.

"Sixteen," said the Captain.

"What is his occupation?" I said.

"He makes faces for clocks in the Big Ben clock factory at La Salle, Illinois," said the Captain.

"How long has he been loafing at Lake Ripley?" I said.

"About two weeks," said the Captain.

"Who has been feeding him?" I said.

"The Lee family," said the Captain.

"Do they vouch for him?" I said.

"They do," said the Captain.

"And are you positive," I said, "that this candidate is indeed the Lost Egg whom we were planning to initiate to-night?"

"He will answer for himself, most esteemable brother," said the Captain.

"Are you the Lost Egg?" I said to the candidate.

"Yes," said Herb, when told to give that answer by his conductor.

"What proof can you give me that you are indeed the Lost Egg?" I said.

Here the Captain spoke up.

"Permit me to answer for the candidate, most esteemable brother," he said, "for he is not as well posted on the subject as I am. In my examination of him in the Outer Chamber of our Castle I discovered that he has goat feathers for hair and further has the feet of a goose."

"Pluck a feather for my examination," I said.

Herb's hair was given a good yank.

"Here is a feather, most esteemable brother," said the Captain, pretending to pass the feather to me.

I pretended to examine the feather. Then I smelt of it.

"It is indeed a goat feather," I said. "I can tell by the smell. And I am satisfied that the candidate is the Lost Egg, as you claim. But, tell me, brother Captain of the Court, is he hard-boiled?"

"I will test him on your orders, most esteemable brother," said the Captain.

"Proceed with the test," I said.

You will understand now why Herb had been

carrying the croquet mallet and the maul. For here the Captain took the mallet and hit the candidate a snappy crack on the back of the bean. I don't mean he tried to pull off any knock-out stuff. Not at all. For, as I say, Mr. Lee had given us our orders not to get rough. But just the same Herb was hit hard enough to make him feel it. The scheme was to make him say "ouch." However, he didn't say "ouch" right away. So we had to do some more work.

"Most esteemable brother," said the Captain to me, "I have tested the candidate with the croquet mallet, as you ordered, and he does not say 'ouch.' What shall I do?"

"Proceed with the test with added vigor," I said, "until he does say 'Ouch.' "

Herb took the hint then.

"Ouch!" said he, before we could get another crack at him.

"He has said 'ouch,' most esteemable brother," said the Captain, "which is proof that he is hard-boiled."

"The result of the test is satisfactory to me," I said. "And accordingly you have my permission to conduct the candidate to our Most Excellent Humpty-Dumpty."

Here the talking-machine record was started

again and the conductor marched the candidate twice around the room, stopping before Humpty-Dumpty's station. Then the music was stopped.

"Cock-a-doodle-doo," said the Captain.

"Cut-cut-ca-daw-cut," said Humpty-Dumpty.

"Here, Most Excellent Humpty-Dumpty," said the Captain, "is the Lost Egg."

Humpty-Dumpty took a squint at the candidate, as I had done, and turned up his nose.

"*This* thing!" said he in disgust. "It looks to me like something the cat dragged in."

Everybody in the room was laughing at Herb, especially the girls he had tried to shine around. And, believe me, in his dizzy outfit he did look like something the cat had dragged in, as Humpty-Dumpty had said.

"It is indeed the Lost Egg, Most Excellent Humpty-Dumpty," said the Captain.

"How do I know it is the Lost Egg?" said Humpty-Dumpty.

"I found him in an ash can in Oglesby, Illinois, and have given his name and history to our esteemed brother, Keeper of the Keys, who is satisfied as to the candidate's identity."

"Is he hard-boiled?" said Humpty-Dumpty.

"I shall test him on your orders, Most Excellent Humpty-Dumpty," said the Captain.

"Proceed with the test," said Humpty-Dumpty.

Golly Ned! You should have seen Herb's knees wabble when the Captain took the big maul. He was thinking of how we had used the croquet mallet on him. And he figured that he was going to get a ten times harder crack with the maul. That was the fun of it.

The Captain let the maul fall to the floor.

"What was that noise?" said Humpty-Dumpty.

"I dropped the maul by accident, Most Excellent Humpty-Dumpty," said the Captain.

Humpty-Dumpty cried out in surprise.

"What!" said he. "You don't mean to tell me that you are going to strike that boy with that big maul?"

"I thought that was your wish, Most Excellent Humpty-Dumpty," said the Captain.

"I should say not," said Humpty-Dumpty. "Why, you might knock him cuckoo. It will be better, I think, to use this baseball bat on him. Here, take it. I shall count three. Are you ready? One, two, *three.*"

What Humpty-Dumpty handed the Captain, instead of a baseball bat, was a feather pillow. And at the third count, when Herb expected to get a biff with a hickory club, he was struck on the back of the neck with the soft pillow. And you should have seen him stagger! It was almost as bad for him, I guess, as getting soaked with the bat. The shock was there just the same.

"The result of the test is satisfactory to me," said Humpty-Dumpty, when Herb had quit staggering in the glad knowledge that his head was still on his shoulders. "I am convinced that he is indeed hard-boiled. So in continuation of his initiation you will take this egg and anoint him on the head."

Now, I haven't said anything about Herb's hair. But he had swell hair. Boy, he sure did love to pet and pat that nice little brush pile of his. And because he loved it so, and was so swelled up over it, is why this part of his initiation was funny to us.

An egg had been fixed up with water in it. The yolk had been blown out through a small hole, I mean, and water had been put in the shell with a nose syringe. Then the holes had been sealed with adhesive tape.

Now the Captain took this egg and squashed it on top of Herb's head. The water from the egg ran down the candidate's face and neck. He didn't like it a bit. And he began to claw the nasty old egg shell out of his pretty hair.

At the same time that the egg had been broken

Humpty-Dumpty had uncorked a bottle of "stink" —I think it was carbon disulphide—and the saturated cork was waved under Herb's nose. The poor kid almost gagged up his stomach. He didn't know for sure what it was that he smelt, but connecting the smell with the broken egg he was pretty sure that he had been plastered on the head with a rotten egg.

"Oh! Oh! Oh! Oh!" said the Captain.

"What is wrong, Captain of the Court?" said Humpty-Dumpty. "Why do you thus cry out and hold your nose?"

"I fear, Most Excellent Humpty-Dumpty," said the Captain, "that the egg I broke on the candidate's head is rotten. For there is a bad smell."

Humpty-Dumpty exercised his nose.

"I should say there is a bad smell," he said, gasping. "Phew! This is awful. What can we do?"

I want to tell you that Herb was doing all *he* could. Boy, he was clawing the stuff out of his hair just as fast as he knew how. When he smelt of his fingers I thought everybody would bust.

"I might soak the candidate's head in a tub of water, Most Excellent Humpty-Dumpty," said the Captain.

"No," said Humpty-Dumpty. "Take off his shoes. His feet will smell so much worse than the rotten egg that we won't notice the egg smell."

I got a chair for the candidate and we made him sit down in the middle of the room. Then his shoes were taken off. But we didn't take off his socks.

"Captain of the Court," said Humpty-Dumpty.

"Yes, Most Excellent Humpty-Dumpty," said the Captain, saluting.

"What seems to be the matter with the candidate's forehead? He seems to be perspiring."

"He is warm and excited, Most Excellent Humpty-Dumpty," said the Captain.

"Proceed then to cool him off," said Humpty-Dumpty.

Here the Captain put the candidate's feet in a foot tub, after which Herb was made to stand up. And there he stood like a big gawk while we poured a pail of ice water into the tub. He tried to get out of the tub after a moment or two, for the water was too co-o-old for him! But he got back in the tub in a jiffy when we hit his toes a crack.

"Most Excellent Humpty-Dumpty," said the Captain, saluting.

"Yes, Captain of the Court," said Humpty-Dumpty.

"The candidate, nicely refreshed, is in the proper position to take the oath."

Herb was now standing first on one foot and then on the other, like a stork. It was a scream to see him.

"Herb Isham," said Humpty-Dumpty, "you will give your name in full and repeat after me——"

This was my cue. And I rapped on the door of the Outer Chamber. Stopping his work, Humpty-Dumpty scowled at me.

"Keeper of the Keys," said he sharply.

"Yes, Most Excellent Humpty-Dumpty," I said, saluting.

"What is the cause of this confusion?"

"There is a messenger without the Outer Gate of our Castle, Most Excellent Humpty-Dumpty."

"A messenger!" said Humpty-Dumpty. "It must be a matter of great importance. We will await the messenger's tidings before we proceed with the initiation."

I rattled the chain and opened the door.

"Most Excellent Humpty-Dumpty," I said, saluting.

"Yes, Keeper of the Keys."

"The messenger is Dick Powell from Oglesby, Illinois. He brings word that there may be some question as to the candidate's sincerity in seeking admittance into our secret order. It even is hinted that he is a spy."

Humpty-Dumpty got up on his ear then.

"Search the candidate!" he roared.

The Captain went through Herb's pockets and found a "planted" letter.

"Most Excellent Humpty-Dumpty," said the Captain, saluting, when he had read the letter.

"Yes, Captain of the Court," said Humpty-Dumpty.

"I have found on the candidate's person, close to his heart, a letter from a lady. And here in the letter's conclusion are many strange hieroglyphics. I see little crosses and circles. These undoubtedly have a hidden meaning. I fear the candidate is indeed a spy."

Now, this wouldn't have been so funny to the kids if Herb hadn't actually gotten some letters from girls down his way. He had flashed two or three of these letters under my nose to let me know how popular he was with the Oglesby fair sex. Yah. Sheik stuff. The damsels all dropped their knitting when *he* breezed into sight in the boulevard. You tell 'em, kid!

"It is but fair to the candidate," said Humpty-Dumpty, "that we give him a chance to defend himself. Herb Isham, what is the meaning of these crosses and circles?"

Herb didn't say anything. He was scared to death, I guess, that we really had one of his loving little letters.

"Most Excellent Humpty-Dumpty," said the Captain, saluting.

"Yes, Captain of the Court," said Humpty-Dumpty.

"The candidate says that the crosses are kisses and the circles hugs."

Humpty-Dumpty scowled at the candidate.

"How very disgusting," said he. "To think that a boy of your age, Herb Isham, should get letters from girls, in which are crosses for kisses and circles for hugs. For all we know to the contrary this letter may be from a married woman. I consider this a very disgraceful situation."

"Most Excellent Humpty-Dumpty," said the Captain, saluting, "the letter is signed Miss —— ——."

"Who is this Miss —— ——?" Humpty-Dumpty inquired of the candidate. "Is she a nice girl?"

Herb didn't say anything. We had him now!

For we had given him the name of one of his girls.

"Most Excellent Humpty-Dumpty," said the Captain, saluting.

"Yes, Captain of the Court."

"I happen to know that this Miss —— —— *is* a nice girl. Possibly she did not show good judgment in putting kisses and hugs into her letter, but that is not a grave offense. As for the candidate, while he may be a bit 'soft' on the girl stuff, I am convinced that he is not a spy."

"Very well," said Humpty-Dumpty, "we will proceed with the initiation. Herb Isham, you will give your name in full and repeat after me: I, Herb Isham—do hereby solemnly promise—to forever keep the dark secrets—of this notable juvenile order—and will do my part hereafter—in a friendly way—in helping to initiate other boys—into the order. Furthermore—I promise—to beg the young ladies—who think so much of me—to discontinue—writing letters to me—containing—kisses and hugs. Cock-a-doodle-doo."

Well, Herb said everything all right, only he kind of stumbled over the part about the kisses and hugs. He didn't like that.

"Having taken the oath," said Humpty-Dumpty to the candidate, "you have only to have the emblem of our order tattooed on your naked breast to become a full-fledged member in good standing. Keeper of the Keys."

"Yes, Most Excellent Humpty-Dumpty," I said, saluting.

"On my orders you will heat the tattooing iron."

I went up to the candidate with a piece of burning rubber, letting the smoke go up his nose.

"The iron is ready, Most Excellent Humpty-Dumpty," I said, saluting.

"Are you sure it isn't too hot?" said Humpty-Dumpty. "We don't want to burn a hole through the candidate."

"I have tested the iron on my rubber shoe," I said, "and it does not set the shoe afire."

"Very well," said Humpty-Dumpty. "Bare the candidate's breast and apply the iron."

Herb squirmed when we started to unbutton his shirt. But it didn't do him any good. And when we had his breast nicely bared we rubbed a piece of ice on him. Then we let the ice slip down inside of his clothes. You should have seen him double over when the cold hunk hit his "tummy."

"My brother," said Humpty-Dumpty, "you are

now a full-fledged member of our lodge, *The Secret Order of Humpty-Dumpty, The Rejuvenated Egg.* Here is the grip and here is the password—fried omelet. Later on you will sign your name and address in the Castle Registration Book."

Here I grabbed some pans that we had handy, along with our other truck, and banged them on the floor.

"Keeper of the Keys," said Humpty-Dumpty.

"Yes, Most Excellent Humpty-Dumpty," I said, saluting.

"What was that noise?"

"The new brother dropped a nickel in the tub, Most Excellent Humpty-Dumpty," I said.

"You say the new brother dropped a nickel in the tub?" said Humpty-Dumpty. "That being the case, make the brother get out of the tub and get down on his hands and knees and find the nickel."

We made Herb get out of the tub. And when he was on his hands and knees we gave him a sharp spat on the seat of his pants with a "clatter" paddle. That made him howl. He thought he was getting killed from the noise the paddle made.

"That, Herb Isham," said Humpty-Dumpty,

helping the candidate to his feet, "completes your initiation into our lodge. You have been fully rejuvenated."

I guess that tells everything. Maybe I haven't told it very good, but I've done the best I know how. As I say, in this story-writing stuff I'm not the clever little pencil pusher that Jerry Todd is.

Since that first initiation we've had other initiations. We have a book called the Castle Registration Book, and in it we have the names of the charter officers, the initiated members and the charter members. The people who are invited to the initiations now, to see the work for the first time, are called honorary members. It's fun to take the Registration Book and look through it. It recalls a lot of good times.

Now, you must believe me when I say that everything I have written down is true. And I tell you what—if ever you are near Lake Ripley in the summer time drop in and see me for a few minutes. Or, if you prefer, stop in at Hi-Lee Cottage and see Mr. and Mrs. Lee and their boy "Beanie." There's a secret about "Beanie" and Jerry Todd, but I can't put you wise here. I'll whisper the secret to you if you come to see me. A lot of boys come to Lake Ripley to see

Mr. Lee. And they all get a warm welcome. I want you to know that.

Remember, Lake Ripley is a mile out of Cambridge. And to give you an idea where Cambridge is on the Wisconsin map, I'll tell you that our lake is twenty-four miles east of Madison, between Madison and Fort Atkinson.

Golly Ned! Wouldn't it be peachy if you could happen around some time when we were having an initiation! You'd get your name in the Castle Registration Book then as an honorary member.

And I guess that's all.

THE END